DEMCO, INC. 38-2931

HADASSAH

Hadassah

The Girl Who Became Queen Esther

TOMMY TENNEY

Adapted from the novel HADASSAH
written by Tommy Tenney with Mark Andrew Olsen

BETHANYHOUSE
MINNEAPOLIS, MINNESOTA

Hadassah: The Girl Who Became Queen Esther
Copyright © 2005
Tommy Tenney

Cover and text illustrations by Dave Kramer
Cover design by Melinda Schumacher

Published by Bethany House Publishers
11400 Hampshire Avenue South
Bloomington, Minnesota 55438

Bethany House Publishers is a division of
Baker Publishing Group, Grand Rapids, Michigan.

Printed in the United States of America

Library of Congress Cataloging-in-Publication Data

Tenney, Tommy, 1956-
    Hadassah : the girl who became Queen Esther / by Tommy Tenney.
        p.   cm.
    Summary: Teen-aged Hadassah, a reluctant candidate for Queen of Persia, feels sorrow at leaving her family but she is eager to have a chance to protect her people from persecution.
    ISBN 0-7642-2738-6 (hardcover : alk. paper)
    [1. Esther, Queen of Persia—Fiction. 2. Kings, queens, rulers, etc.—Fiction.
3. Jews—Fiction. 4. Iran—History—To 640—Fiction.] I. Title.
    PZ7.T26394Had   2005
    [Fic]—dc22   2004020197

TOMMY TENNEY, along with his wife, Jeannie, has been a world traveler for more than thirty years. An avid reader and relentless researcher, Tenney is a highly acclaimed inspirational speaker and bestselling nonfiction author with combined sales of over three million copies. He has here turned his hand to fiction and the captivating story of Esther.

Tenney says, "In attempting to understand and more fully appreciate my wife, the queen of my life, I discovered Esther's fascinating story. Totally powerless, she fully prepared herself to finally maneuver a powerful king toward a destiny larger than either of them."

The Tenneys have three daughters, and Tommy had them in mind when plans were being made to adapt *Hadassah* for younger readers. The family makes their home in Louisiana.

For more information, you may access:
Hadassah-onenightwiththeking.com
TommyTenney.com

HADASSAH'S EIGHTEENTH BIRTHDAY CELEBRATION
was coming to a close, and she leaned on the windowsill
overlooking the darkened courtyard of her Persian home. In
her hand was a beautiful medallion inscribed with a six-
pointed star. She held it up in the moonlight, allowing it to
catch the silvery rays, and she remembered the very first
time she had ever seen this medallion.

It was at the time of another one of her birthdays,
many years before when she was a small child, and the
memories of that long-ago day made her heart feel like it
was being squeezed in her chest. She'd had no hint way
back then of the incredible changes that would come to her
or the terrible losses she would face before that birthday
was hardly over. She couldn't keep her thoughts from drift-
ing back to that moonlit night, one very much like this
one. . . .

HADASSAH WAS SO EXCITED SHE COULD BARELY stand still. It was her seventh birthday, and her mother was getting ready to give her something. Hadassah could tell it must be something very special because of the way her mother was holding the gift carefully in her hands.

"Oh, Mama," Hadassah exclaimed, "I can hardly wait! Please, please, *please* let me see what you are holding!" She looked up into her mother's gentle brown eyes and smiled as convincingly as she could.

"All right, my dearest, here it is," her mother said, laughing at Hadassah's enthusiasm. She opened her hands, and there lay the most beautiful gold medallion Hadassah had ever seen. She very carefully reached out, and her mother laid the shining pendant into her cupped hands.

Hadassah couldn't even speak as she gazed at the medallion. Without understanding at the time everything it meant or how valuable it was, she knew even then it was the most special gift she had ever received. After staring at it a long time, she looked up again at her mother. "It's got a star on it," she said. "And it's got . . . it's got six points on it, too," she added, counting them with one finger.

"Yes," said Hadassah's father as he walked over to join them. "That star represents the Promised Land, the land of Israel," he explained as he put a hand on her dark curly hair. "Even though our ancestors have not lived there for many years, your mother and I love the land of our Jewish heritage."

Her mother added, "Many years ago your great-great-grandmother brought this medallion with her on the journey all the way from the Promised Land here to Persia, where we live now." She put her arm around Hadassah's shoulder and looked at the gleaming star shape in her daughter's hands. "Our forefathers were greatly outnumbered in the battle, and the King of Babylon captured most of our people, the Hebrews, including your great-grandmother. He forced them to march a very long time until they finally arrived here in the land of Persia."

"Was that king mean to Great-grandmother?" Hadassah questioned her parents.

Her father answered, "That king was determined to rule every country bordering on Babylon. He did not want to leave many of our people, the Jews, where they were in case they would rise up against him and take the land back." Her father moved his hand from Hadassah's head to her shoulder as he said, "But Babylon was then conquered by Persia, and there have been several kings since King Nebuchadnezzar invaded Israel, and they mostly have let us live our own lives and have not allowed anybody to bother us Jews living here."

Hadassah looked again at her medallion and took it over to the window to catch the evening light. Even though she was just a child, she could tell it was very old and very valuable.

"Your father and I want you to have the pendant now because you are our bright star," Mama said, joining her at the window and giving her a hug. "But we will put it away in a safe place for you to wear when you grow up," she added.

Hadassah looked at her parents with her most pleading expression. "Oh, please, please, *please*," she begged again, "could I just wear it tonight? Just this one time? And then you may save it in a very special safe place," she promised, nodding her head solemnly.

Her mother and father looked at each other with a certain loving look. Then her mother laughed again and reached out to smooth Hadassah's hair back from her face. "Yes, my dear, you may wear it this one night," she agreed with another hug.

Hadassah looked at the medallion once more, then lifted the chain so it could hang around her neck. "Thank you, Papa and Mama, for this beautiful gift. I will treasure it always."

Later, when the sun had set and it was dark, her mother led Hadassah into the back room and to her corner pallet, and her father came to pray the wonderful Hebrew blessing called the *Shema* over her. "'Hear, O Israel: The Lord our God, the Lord is one,'" her father began. "'Love the Lord your God with all your heart and with all your soul and with all your strength.'" Hadassah wasn't sure exactly what all those words meant, but she knew she wanted to love God with all her heart. Soon she was snuggled under her blankets to sleep, the necklace around her neck and her hand curled around the medallion.

Neither Hadassah nor her parents had noticed the Persian soldier lurking just outside their courtyard gate, watching them and listening in on their conversation. When Hadassah's mother blew out the last candle and the windows were all dark, he slinked away into the shadows on an evil mission—a welcome report to his commander who was on his own evil mission of vengeance.

Later that night something suddenly awakened Hadassah. She sat up on her pallet in the dark and frantically tried to imagine what the loud, frightening noises could mean.

"Mama! Mama!" she called again and again. But no one answered her. It all was very terrifying and confusing. She could barely see anything in the darkness, but it looked like some wicked-looking men were crashing around in the house, shouting and breaking things in the front room.

Through the door of her bedroom, she saw the glint of moonlight on an upraised sword, then a flash as the weapon swept downward. She heard screams—was that her mother's voice? She wasn't sure. Then Hadassah finally realized she was screaming herself.

As one of the intruders ran out the front door, the moonlight gave her a glimpse of a strange symbol on his cloak. It looked like . . . like some kind of twisted cross. She was too terrified to give it another thought.

In the chaos no one seemed to see or hear the little girl as she clutched her blanket around her and whimpered in the darkness. Hadassah hardly dared lift her head, but it finally seemed like the wicked men were all outside the house, laughing cruelly and shouting to each other in the courtyard.

The men must have had horses, because Hadassah could hear their hoofbeats and frightened whinnies as they galloped through the gate. Finally it seemed like the wicked raiders might be gone. But Hadassah didn't move a muscle. She squeezed her eyes tightly closed and feverishly hoped this was all simply a bad dream. But she was afraid to open her eyes for fear of finding out it *wasn't* just a dream.

The next thing Hadassah felt was unusual warmth on her face, and she opened her eyes to see flickering light against the wall next to her. Then the blaze from a fire leaped into the room where she was huddled in the corner. Even though the flames were licking everything around her, she was so frightened she couldn't even move.

But when a flame started up her nightclothes, she scrambled to her feet, ran across the room, and leaped through the doorway ringed in fire.

CHAPTER TWO

HADASSAH LAY AS STILL AS DEATH IN A STRANGE BED
and unfamiliar house, barely conscious.

The fiery pain on her legs felt better when someone
carefully smoothed what smelled like goat's butter on them.
But she kept her eyes closed tight when anyone came into
the room. She couldn't bear to think about where she was
or why she was here and not at home with her mother and
father.

"Oh, my little Hadassah," she often heard a man's voice
say and could feel a hand stroking her hair back from her
forehead. But she knew it was not her father's voice, and it
just took too much effort to try to respond. Mercifully,
Hadassah slept most of each day as well as the nights.

"'Hear, O Israel: the Lord our God, the Lord is
one. . . .'" Hadassah listened to the familiar words as if
from a long ways away. Gradually, as she was able to concentrate on what the words meant, she slowly opened her
eyes. At first she couldn't see very much at all. Then finally
she was able to make out the face next to her bed.

"Uncle Mordecai," she whispered through lips that felt

stiff and dry. Though he had only occasionally visited Hadassah's home, she recognized her cousin, whom she called "Uncle" since he was quite a bit older than she.

"Shhh, my sweet," he gently said. "You are here with me now, and I'm going to help you get well again." The young man lifted her head so he could hold a cup of cold water to her mouth. Some of it dribbled down the side of her face, and he carefully wiped it away. He held her hand and continued to stroke her hair.

"Uncle Mordecai," she tried again, more clearly this time. "Why am I here? Why am I with you?"

"Don't try to talk now, Hadassah," he said, gently laying her back on the bed. "I'll tell you about it soon. But right now we need to concentrate on getting you well again."

Over the next weeks and months, Hadassah gradually learned that her parents had been killed that dreadful night, and that her Uncle Mordecai had arrived on the scene just in time to catch her as she came through the fiery doorway.

As Hadassah wept in his arms, she asked through her tears, "But Papa prayed the Shema over me that very night before . . . before it all happened. Why didn't God take care of them—why didn't He protect them?"

Uncle Mordecai held her close and said, "I have the same questions, dear little Hadassah, and I lie in my bed at night and ask the Lord over and over why this has happened. I do not have an answer for you yet, and it's possible you and I will never know the reason. But what I do know is that our Creator also loves what He has created, and He loves you. You could have died in the fire, and yet you are here with me now. God may have a purpose for your life that we don't understand yet, a special job for you to do. Like our ancestor Job we can say, 'Though He slay me, yet will I trust Him.'"

"I miss my parents so much," Hadassah said, her voice broken with grief. "It's hard to trust God."

"Yes, but I think He knows that, too, and He will help your faith to become strong and sure as your body and your soul recover from this terrible ordeal," Mordecai said, rocking her back and forth in his arms as he comforted her.

"I will love you and take care of you always," Mordecai promised after they had not spoken for a while.

Hadassah believed him, and she drifted off to sleep again.

❦

Though her uncle Mordecai was just a young man, after a while it seemed easy and natural for her to call him "Papa." She would listen for his voice calling her name from the gate when he returned home after work, and she would go running to meet him. He would swing her up in his arms and around in a circle, and they both would laugh with joy and the excitement of life.

Hadassah loved to sit on his lap in the evenings while

he told her fascinating stories about how their nation, the land of the Israelites, had been settled by the Jewish Patriarchs, Abraham, Isaac and Jacob. He described Sarah and Rachel and Rebecca, women who had been strong and faithful to God even during heartbreaking and difficult times like the one through which Hadassah had lived. He told about the Jews, also known as Hebrews, being driven from their land by wicked men—men like those who had taken the life of her parents. But he also told her that God was with them here in Persia, and that He would be with Hadassah and help her to be brave and strong like those other women of long ago.

I want to be like Sarah, like Rachel and Rebecca, Hadassah would think dreamily as she drifted off to sleep at night. *I want to be brave like Mama was....* Sometimes tears would creep out from under her eyelids. But she cried only softly into her pillow so Papa Mordecai would not hear her and worry.

Papa Mordecai had a delightful housekeeper named Rachel, and she came to their home every day to cook and clean and teach Hadassah how to grow into a proper Jewish woman. Rachel had a grandson named Jesse who was only a little older than Hadassah. Since Mordecai was very protective of Hadassah and did not allow her to go outside their courtyard very often and only when he was with her, Rachel often brought Jesse along to the house so they could play together. They were good friends, laughing and shouting in the courtyard and chasing each other around the fig tree that grew in the center.

"Can't catch me," Jesse teased as he ran around the circle.

"I'll bet I can!" Hadassah called back as she jumped over a bench and nearly knocked him to the ground.

"You two be careful!" Rachel scolded from the doorway as she came out to empty a bowl of water on the roots of the fig tree. But she couldn't help but smile as she shook her head at the two children laughing and racing around once more.

Jesse and Hadassah each passed more birthdays and got to be twelve and fourteen years old. He had to spend more and more time with his studies at the synagogue school for Jewish boys, so he was not able to come to the house with his grandmother as often as he had done in the past. Rachel tried to keep Hadassah busy with housework, cooking, and mending, but Hadassah often found herself bored and looking for things to occupy her mind and her hands. She looked forward to the evenings when her papa came back from work. If he was not too tired, Mordecai and Hadassah would sit together at the table in the candlelight, and he began teaching her to read and write like Jesse.

Hadassah knew it was very unusual for girls in Persia to be taught reading and writing, and Papa Mordecai told her she must be very careful to keep it a secret or it could make things difficult for her—and for him—among others in

their community. He explained that women were expected to keep their households in order and raise children. "You could be viewed with suspicion if it were known that you could read and write on your own." She secretly wondered if any of those female ancestors she so admired had been taught as Papa Mordecai was teaching her.

Hadassah did love reading the stories of her people, the Israelites, and of the Promised Land for herself. Hadassah daydreamed about doing something wonderful for God, maybe even going to Israel someday.

"'In the beginning,'" she carefully read out loud, one finger pointing to each Hebrew word in the scroll Mordecai had borrowed from the synagogue, "'God created the heavens and the earth.'" Mordecai smiled from across the table at her.

From the corner where she was making bread, Rachel muttered, "Mark my words, all this reading is going to get her into a whole packet of trouble." But Mordecai just shrugged and Hadassah rolled her eyes toward Rachel's back as the two shared a grin.

During the daytime Rachel expertly taught Hadassah how to clean house, wash dishes and clothes, and cook meals. Hadassah was very proud of the first supper she fixed all by herself, and her papa announced it was very good.

"See, I told you," said Rachel loudly, "the girl should concentrate on preparing herself to be a wife and mother.

What is she going to do with scrolls and reading, may I ask?"

Since there was no use trying to convince Rachel otherwise, Mordecai just winked at Hadassah and helped himself to more of the savory lamb stew. "You are right, Rachel, Hadassah will make a wonderful wife someday. Just not very soon. She has a lot more learning to get—from both of us!" Rachel turned her head from one to the other and glared. Mordecai and Hadassah couldn't help but burst out laughing.

"We'll see whose 'preparation' is needed most," she grumbled. But when she saw they were still laughing, she finally joined in.

The day Hadassah came across the story of Abraham and Sarah, she nearly knocked the table over as she jumped up in excitement.

"Look, Rachel, here is where it tells about Sarah!" she exclaimed, pointing to the parchment. "She probably was even older than you when she first had a baby!" Hadassah added mischievously, watching Rachel's expression.

"Oh, go on with you! I'm not that old," Rachel said crossly. But Hadassah could see a twinkle in the woman's eye, and she came over to have a look at the strange hieroglyphics Hadassah's finger was pointing to.

Rachel shook her head. "Well, I believe you," she said as she went back to her work. "Tell me when you come to my ancestor Rachel. I'd like you to read her story to me."

CHAPTER THREE

AS HADASSAH PASSED HER FIFTEENTH BIRTHDAY, SHE was feeling more and more lonely and tired of her life. *I only see Papa and Rachel,* she complained to herself. Jesse hardly ever came over anymore, and now that they were almost grown up, it didn't feel quite right chasing each other around like they used to do. Jesse sometimes was able to bring a scroll from school for her to read, and she liked that. But it didn't happen nearly often enough to keep her from feeling bored, restless, and too confined.

Papa Mordecai still did not want her to leave their walled courtyard, especially not on her own. Every time she asked about going someplace, he explained that it was too dangerous for a Jewish girl in this land of Persia, particularly one whose increasing beauty could attract unwanted attention. Hadassah couldn't help but feeling pleased when he mentioned her looks. When she occasionally caught a glimpse of herself reflected in the water of their well, she thought she knew what her papa was talking about. Her long, silky dark hair and eyes framed in thick, black eyelashes against her smooth, fair skin did indeed seem attractive to her, even though she hadn't seen that many women for comparison. But she gave it little thought except when Mordecai brought it up or when Jesse seemed to stare at her with a certain look in his eyes. She would blush, look away, and change the subject, though it made her feel kind of good inside.

Even though their new young King Xerxes seemed to carry no ill will toward the Jews, Mordecai went on to tell her when she was once more agitating to go out, he still was worried. What if the same wicked men who killed her parents should cross paths with Hadassah? If any of those raiders knew she was still alive and possibly able to identify them, they certainly would want to do away with her, he warned her sternly.

"Oh, Papa," she started to argue, but one look at his face convinced her that she would not change his mind.

Late that night, after Mordecai had gone to sleep, Hadassah slipped from her bed out into the courtyard and up the rickety ladder to the roof of their house. She carefully made her way to the edge, where she could peer down into the street. In spite of the late hour, people were still walking about, and Hadassah kept her head low in case someone might glance up and see her. How she envied them their freedom! She stayed out in the cool night air as long as she dared, then silently crept down the ladder and back to her bed. She stared up into the darkness for a long time before she got to sleep.

It had been weeks since any visits from Jesse, but the next morning he showed up again with Rachel.

As the two young people sat at the table, Hadassah asked Jesse lots of questions about school, about his friends, about life on the other side of the gate leading out to the street.

"Oh," she exclaimed after he had described the outdoor market near the palace. "I so would like to get out and see things like you get to do!"

"Oh no, Hadassah," Jesse answered, shaking his head. "I agree with your father about this. Mordecai feels it's too dangerous for you to be out there among strangers. You're too pretty. . . ." He stopped talking and turned kind of red.

"Oh, there are lots of pretty girls out there, I'm sure," she argued.

He shook his head. "No, Hadassah, believe me. You would get too much attention." He turned to look directly at her. "If you must know, I have never seen a girl as beautiful as you are."

Hadassah knew Jesse was embarrassed, so she said a quiet "Thank you" and turned away for a while.

"I have an idea," she exclaimed suddenly. "I'll dress up like a boy—like you! Then I'll look the same as any other kid running around the streets!" She jumped up enthusiastically and started walking back and forth, thinking through her plans. She didn't notice Jesse shaking his head back and forth or Rachel muttering over in the corner.

"No, Hadassah—there's no way it will work," he said,

finally getting her to pay attention to what he was saying. "One look at your face—"

"Which I will have mostly covered with the end of the headdress," she put in, dismissing his concerns with a wave of her hand. "I can even wipe some mud on my cheeks—"

"You're crazy," Jesse said, sounding disgusted. But Hadassah noticed he seemed just a bit thoughtful.

"Come on, Hadassah," Jesse finally said. "I've learned a new game at synagogue school, and I'll teach you how to play it."

The two moved toward the door into the courtyard as Rachel stared after them, looking thoughtful, too. Jesse was explaining the rules to her. "It's actually more of a school test than a game, but our teacher, the rabbi, likes to think he's tricking us into it by calling it a game." He bent down to pick up a stick.

"See," he said, bending over to scratch a Hebrew letter on the ground, "the first person picks a word, and the next person has to use it to start a sentence. . . ." And soon they were both busy playing the new game.

But Hadassah couldn't get her idea about a disguise out of her mind, and eventually she lost the game to Jesse.

After Jesse and Rachel had gone home, Hadassah lay in bed thinking again about that enticing world outside their courtyard gate. How she would love to explore it without Mordecai or Rachel hurrying her along home from some brief errand.

It was only a few days later when Hadassah noticed Rachel had brought a mysterious-looking bundle with her when she came to work. "What's that?" Hadassah wanted to know as Rachel tucked it into a corner.

"Just wait, my impatient one. You'll know all in good time," she said. "You get your bed folded up and the court-yard swept, and then I'll tell you."

Hadassah quickly got her work done, thinking all the while about Rachel's curious bundle. "All right, Mama Rachel," she said, knowing the woman liked Hadassah to call her that, "I'm finished now. What—"

"Patience, my love," Rachel cautioned with a smile. "*I'm* not finished yet. Here, help me hang this washing, and then I'll tell you." The two soon had the laundry draped carefully over bushes and the courtyard walls.

"All right," Rachel finally said, leading Hadassah over to the bundle. "Now I'll show you." She opened it and laid out a selection of male garments, probably ones that belonged to her grandson Jesse. "Actually, my dear, I don't think it's right for Mordecai to keep you cooped up here like this. I have been talking with him about it, and I haven't gotten him to agree yet. But I will." And then she proceeded to help Hadassah dress in her new identity.

First Rachel wet down Hadassah's long hair from a

pitcher of well water and then wrapped it tightly around her head inside a long linen strip. Then she topped the whole thing with a shepherd's leather hat with a brim. She pulled out a loose-fitting robe and some worn sandals. They were a little big for Hadassah's feet, but she was not going to complain.

Hadassah's heart was beating with excitement, and she twirled to present herself to Rachel. "How do I look?"

Rachel frowned uncertainly. "I don't know, Hadassah. You still look awfully . . . well, awfully girlish." She went outside and returned with a handful of dirt that she mixed with some water and rubbed on Hadassah's face.

"You're always telling me to wash my face!" Hadassah joked as Rachel stepped back to examine her work.

Rachel nodded and smiled a bit uncertainly, then asked, "Would you let me send Jesse along with you?"

But Hadassah was already vigorously shaking her head no. "It won't be the same if I have someone with me," she said. "I'll be all right, Mama Rachel," Hadassah assured her as convincingly as she could.

"Well, don't speak to anyone," Rachel warned. "If anyone hears your voice . . ." But Hadassah was already hurrying away toward the door. She turned back to nod her agreement with all Rachel's warnings and instructions, then waved good-bye.

"Thanks, Mama Rachel. I'll be back before you know it," she called over her shoulder, knowing she must be

home before Papa Mordecai returned from work.

She lifted the latch on the gate, turned to wave once more to Rachel—who was looking both worried and excited—and slipped through to the street. Hadassah was alone in the city for the first time in her life.

⚜

Oh, it was so exciting! Hadassah felt free and happy—and maybe a little bit scared—as she started up the busy street toward the king's palace. She knew that was where Papa Mordecai worked every day as one of the royal scribes. He was one of the secretaries who wrote down all the things the king wanted done each day, and it was both important and tedious at the same time. Those instructions were distributed each day to the people who were to carry them out. Royal scribes also recorded a daily diary of all the happenings around the court, whether important or ordinary. The scrolls, known as the Chronicles of the Persian Kings, were collected and saved in the royal vault, Mordecai had told her.

Hadassah was sure her papa would never recognize her dressed like she was, but she was going to be extra careful not to get too near to where he sat. As she came close to the large, beautiful palace, she stopped to look at the entrance across the way.

"That is where my table and chair are located," Mordecai

had explained to her when he talked to her about his work, *"right under the mighty arch of Xerxes."*

"There he is!" Hadassah almost said the words out loud, but she remembered in time that if anyone heard her speak, they would know she was not a boy.

Hadassah walked around the area in front of the palace, keeping a careful eye on Mordecai as he worked over his parchments with quill in hand. She also had to stay out of the way of soldiers on horseback, goats wandering around their owners' stalls, and mothers chasing after rambunctious children.

"How about a nice fresh pomegranate," called a merchant sitting in front of a well-stocked stall. He held out the delicious-looking fruit to Hadassah, but she had no money and shook her head silently. She thought he looked at her rather curiously, and she hurried away. Maybe her disguise wasn't as good as she had hoped.

She rushed around a corner and out of sight of the merchant, then slowed to enjoy the aroma of a roasting chicken on a fire spit across the plaza. Another merchant's awning sheltered a display of fragrant spices, and another rather ornate booth was hung with jewelry and silks in beautiful colors. A lovely pale blue fabric caught her eye, and she was moving toward it when she remembered a boy wouldn't likely be interested in anything like that.

She backed up quickly and bumped right into someone. She whirled to get out of the way—and there was Jesse!

"What do you want?" she grumped crossly under her breath.

"Nothing. Just wanted to make sure you're safe," he answered with a grin.

She felt like stamping her foot at him, but she remembered in time that would look too girlish. "Well, I'm just fine," she muttered, still keeping her voice low.

"Okay, if you're just fine, what's the way back to your house?" he asked knowingly.

Hadassah looked around slowly, but she soon realized there were half a dozen streets fanning out from the square before the palace, and now they all looked the same to her. She groaned inwardly and turned back to Jesse. "Well, don't just stand there gloating, you big goat. Why don't you tell me?"

"I'm sorry," he said, a teasing grin on his face as he cupped a hand around his ear. "Did you say *help* you?"

Hadassah knew when she'd been outwitted, so she shrugged and said, "All right, then help me."

Jesse turned and gestured for her to follow him. He

began to run with long loping strides, and Hadassah grabbed up her robe from around her legs and took off after him as fast as she could. She was desperate not to lose sight of Jesse's back through all the throngs of people. Soon they came to a kind of clearing in the crowd, and she caught up to him, panting and breathless from the unusual activity. She was not used to running.

"Where are we going?" she gasped out. She was sure they weren't headed for home.

"Since we're here already, I'm going to show you something," he said. He turned and headed off again, ducking under a stand selling roasted figs and nuts without even looking back to make sure she was following him. They soon were climbing a steep embankment behind the stand and arrived at its top, high above the crowded market square.

Hadassah gasped as she turned to look at the awesome view over the city. She gasped again as she saw Jesse, elbows back, launch himself forward toward the edge of the steep bank they had just climbed. She was sure he was going to kill himself! But at the last second he leaped into the air, his legs and arms pumping. She ran to see what had happened to him and found him below her, face down on the back of one of the giant half-eagle, half-lion statues flanking the porticoes of the palace.

He sat up and waved to Hadassah to join him, but she shook her head vigorously.

"Shall I call you Hadassah the Mouse?" he shouted up

to her. She knew enough of Jesse's teasing to know his new nickname would follow her around for years. But what if she couldn't jump far enough?

Without stopping to think it over any longer, Hadassah found herself backing up, then running forward, planting her foot on the edge and vaulting into the air. For one glorious moment she felt as light and free as a bird.

An instant later her shins painfully hit the side of the statue, and she was scrambling to hold on to her precarious position. Then a hand reached for hers and pulled her up. Hadassah was sitting behind Jesse, astride the beast as if they were riding it.

Hadassah quickly looked to see if they were in view of Mordecai's place by the palace gate, but they were beyond his line of vision. She gazed around at all the turbaned heads spread out below them, the canopies and livestock stretched in a dizzying sea of movement and color.

"Oh, Jesse," she said breathlessly. "I have never had such an adventure in my whole life!" He hiked up one leg and turned around to face her. He reached out and pulled off the shepherd's hat, brushed the grime from her cheeks, and let her hair fall free of its cloth wrapping.

"There," he said. "You look like a girl again." And a moment later he leaned forward and kissed her lips.

Hadassah's hands flew to her burning cheeks, and she suddenly felt shy, fearful, and happy all at the same time. She took one look at his face, then quickly swung her leg over and

slid down off the statue. The soles of her feet stung. Jesse hit
the ground behind her and returned the hat and length of
linen cloth. She quickly wrapped her head up as best she
could, squashed the hat on top, and they took off again.

Jesse led them to a certain street opening off the square,
and Hadassah soon recognized it as the one she had walked
up that morning from home. Now running downhill
increased their speed, and Hadassah once more had the
sensation of flying.

An old woman beating a rug outside her gate stopped
to stare curiously at Hadassah, and the girl realized she was
not running as boys did. She looked at Jesse and began to
swing her arms and plant her feet solidly like he was doing.

Hadassah almost ran into his back. Stopping beside
him, she looked around and realized they were at her
home. She stared at the courtyard wall, the same one she
looked at every day—but this time from the outside. She
flashed a smile of thanks to Jesse and stepped inside the
gate.

Rachel of course was waiting to hear all about it, and
she was very relieved and glad Jesse had found Hadassah.
And, it turned out, Hadassah was glad, too.

CHAPTER FOUR

WHEN MORDECAI RETURNED FROM WORK THAT EVE-
ning, Hadassah thought she caught him eyeing her curiously a couple of times. But she couldn't be sure. She
decided she would leave her papa to Rachel and let her
convince him that his little girl was growing up and needed
to get out on her own occasionally.

Rachel must have been successful, for every once in a
while she brought her bundle to the house and fixed Hadassah up in her disguise for exploration of the fascinating
world outside the gate. Sometimes Jesse was able to join
her on those outings, but not always.

One of those times when Jesse couldn't come, Hadassah was up in the plaza near the palace and heard a commotion in front of one of the merchant's stands. Her heart
beat wildly as she crept closer, holding the end of her head
wrap around her face.

What she discovered was a group of soldiers screaming
at the merchant, calling him a Jew-pig and scattering his
merchandise on the ground while one of them held him
against the ground with his foot and poised spear. The

beautiful silks and velvets Hadassah remembered from her previous expedition were now trampled and dirty in the dust of the plaza.

"How dare you treat me so insolently, you scum of the earth!" shouted the one who looked like their leader. "Don't you know I have the ear of King Xerxes himself?" He kicked the poor frightened man, who doubled up in pain, then tried to say something in his own defense.

"I . . . I was just finishing with another customer—"

But the brutal soldier gave him another well-placed kick and shouted for him to hold his tongue.

"I am Haman the Agagite," he bent to hiss into the face of the shaking Hebrew. "Your precious King Saul nearly destroyed my ancestors back in Israel, but he wasn't totally successful. He didn't kill everyone, and those ancestors have vowed revenge, which I plan to complete before I die." He finished off this speech with another kick. The other soldiers laughed viciously.

Hadassah noticed an insignia carved into one of the square front posts holding up the merchant's canopy. *It looks like something. . . .* Hadassah tried to remember where she had seen that design before. Then it came to her like a thunderbolt from heaven. *It's like the six-pointed star on my medallion,* she thought in amazement. *The one I got from someone—it must have been my mother—on my birthday! I wonder what happened to it? Is that sign on the post the reason this . . . this Haman knows the man is Jewish?*

While she was thinking about the long-forgotten medallion and its design, Haman snatched out his sword and slashed at the star on the post. "I've got a better sign for you," he snarled. He took a dagger from his belt and scraped the post smooth. He drew a line down, then one across its midpoint. Everyone around grew very still as Haman stepped closer to finish his diagram. At the end of each line, he carved a short line to its right.

Haman stepped back to admire his work.

Hadassah nearly cried out aloud as that same insignia flashed across her memory—it was the one she had glimpsed as a little girl the night her parents were killed! *The twisted cross.*

Trembling, Hadassah drew the cloth more tightly around her face and slowly withdrew from the crowd. She must not attract any attention to herself, or this evil Haman . . . But she couldn't even finish the thought as she turned down her own street and hurried for home.

Hadassah didn't dare tell Papa Mordecai about what she had seen and heard that afternoon, but she decided that was her last adventure on her own. It was simply too dangerous.

The weeks, months, and even years slowly rolled by, with most days seeming just the same as the one before.

After her work with Rachel was finished in the afternoons, Hadassah turned to her studies. Rather than simply trying to entertain herself with reading and writing as she had when she was younger, she was now throwing herself fully into learning what she could from the occasional borrowed scroll, writing down her thoughts and feelings on scraps of parchment Mordecai brought home for her. Most of these she hid inside her bedroll—they were too private for anyone else's eyes. Deep within she still yearned for adventure, but most of the time she had learned to be fairly content. When she thought about what could have happened to her, she was very grateful to Mordecai for rescuing her from tragedy that day so long ago and for fully receiving her into his home as if she were his own daughter.

Hadassah was sitting at the table rolling out another batch of Rachel's unleavened bread when Mordecai returned home unusually early. He looked rather flushed and excited, and Hadassah stopped, her hands covered in flour, to stare at him.

"I have been invited to a royal banquet with the king!" he exclaimed, tossing his outer tunic over a nearby windowsill. "Everyone in the city has been invited. It's going to last for seven days," he added, looking from Rachel to Hadassah expectantly.

"Please, Papa, please take me with you," Hadassah asked before she hardly had time to think. "You said everyone is invited," she added when he hesitated.

"You don't want to be at that banquet, Hadassah," he argued. "It will be crowded and noisy, maybe even some drunken brawls."

"But you will be there to take care of me," Hadassah insisted.

"No, no, my dear," Mordecai said, shaking his head slowly back and forth. "You don't know all the questions I'd have to answer if I came in with a beautiful young girl like you. And if I explained you are my daughter, they'd ask even more questions since they know I've never married. . . ." He paused, still shaking his head. "No, it's just too complicated, maybe even dangerous."

"Then I'll go as a boy," Hadassah said quickly.

Mordecai sat down heavily on his stool, his expression grim.

"I've done it before," Hadassah explained, looking quickly to Rachel for support. Rachel stood in the corner, arms crossed over her chest, nodding her head. Mordecai looked between the two, sighed, and shrugged his shoulders in resignation.

"How can I win an argument with two women?" he asked, lifting his palms heavenward.

Gleefully Hadassah knew she had won. She would be going to a banquet, the first one in her entire life!

As it turned out, Mordecai was able to talk Hadassah

into attending only the last evening of the banquet. She and Rachel began working on her disguise hours before Mordecai would be returning for her. This time her boy's outfit had to be special, not just the rough robes of a Persian street urchin. Rachel had borrowed a length of blue velvet to wrap Hadassah's hair in, and a brightly striped tunic over everything finished off her disguise.

Rachel watched from the gate as the two left for the banquet, and she murmured Jewish blessings on them till they were out of earshot. Hadassah's excitement grew with every step as they joined the stream of revelers heading up the street. The setting sun created colors of fire behind the royal palace.

As the crowds grew thicker, Mordecai reached for Hadassah's hand in a grip so tight it almost hurt. The two were swept along, right up to the portico and through the massive arch near where Mordecai sat with his parchments and quill each day. Hadassah noticed her feet were no longer walking on sand, and she looked down to see the most beautiful marble flooring with an intricate gold-veined pattern throughout. Thick green foliage and beautiful flowers lined the marble walkway.

Suddenly the crowd parted around a beautiful blue pool, its surface reflecting the desert sky as flawlessly as glass.

A moment later they were in front of a second stone arch, this one looking twice as tall and imposing. Hadassah stared up at its size and grandeur, her mouth nearly hanging open.

"Try not to look too awestruck," Mordecai said urgently, his voice low. "It makes you more noticeable." Hadassah quickly tried to change her expression to seem as if she were used to coming to the palace every day. But her heart continued to pound with her excitement and curiosity.

"That huge marble building," said Mordecai, pointing, "is where King Xerxes' throne is located and where he holds court. No one can approach him without an invitation or the person risks getting himself killed. If the king does not hold out his scepter to the one approaching the throne . . ." Mordecai paused, then ran the side of his hand across his throat with a meaningful look.

In spite of her excitement, Hadassah felt a shiver of fear run through her.

Then they were at the central hall, where the banquet was being held, walking between a row of columns so enormous Hadassah couldn't keep herself from tipping her head back to gape at the tops of them. Huge tapestries hung on purple cords between the columns, woven of white and violet threads and fastened with silver rings.

She felt Mordecai's eyes on her, and he smiled but gave a little shake of his head. Hadassah immediately tried to adjust her face to an ordinary expression. Mordecai led her over to some tables piled high with food of all kinds— braised geese, baked ducks, and whole roasted chickens.

But on another table Hadassah saw the carcass of a half-eaten pig, and she turned away toward something that looked more appetizing. And of course Hebrew dietary laws did not allow for eating pork. Another table sagged beneath the weight of enormous golden goblets of wine.

Mordecai and Hadassah helped themselves to some chicken before moving on toward the far end of the building. Then through the crowd she saw a massive stairway leading up to a high platform holding more tapestry hangings and a gathering of golden couches. Large palm fronds waved slowly over those reclining on them.

And there was King Xerxes! His couch was higher than the rest, and a half-circle of guards, scimitars held at the ready in their fists, formed behind him. He had broad shoulders, dark hair, and a short beard, and he was wearing a golden robe that draped down over the couch on either side.

Suddenly a commotion broke out, and a drunken reveler stumbled to the bottom step leading up to the king. "To His Majesty's health!" he shouted, waving his goblet and spilling wine all over himself. The king smiled lazily down on the man, but then the man started stumbling up the steps, in his drunken state no doubt assuming the king's smile was an invitation.

The crowd gasped, then turned absolutely still as two guards rushed to haul the unfortunate reveler away.

"What are they going to do to him?" Hadassah finally

croaked out, but Mordecai silenced her with a grim look, telling her more than his words would have. She remembered Mordecai's gesture across his throat, and her knees went weak with terror.

From his position high above the crowd, the king raised his own goblet above his head and shook his head with a rueful smile over the man's obvious folly.

Immediately a whole sea of goblets were waved in response to the king, and thousands of voices began to shout "Xerxes! Xerxes!" until it became a single unison chant. The king motioned for the group on the platform with him to move in closer, and after a discussion, the king stood to his feet and raised his goblet once more. The crowd again went silent.

"Vashti! Queen Vashti!" he shouted into the stillness. Every voice in the great hall took up the chant. A group of guards rushed down the stairway and through the crowd that quickly parted in front of them.

Mordecai reluctantly explained to Hadassah's curious look at him that the crowd was calling for the queen to come to be paraded before them. "These drunken revelers want to see her," he said, sounding troubled, "like a prize horse." His voice trailed off, and Hadassah wondered what he wasn't telling her.

After a short while the group of guards came striding back through the throng, and Hadassah strained to see over the shoulders arrayed in front of her for a glimpse of the queen. But she saw only the armed men marching in step back up to the king. The crowd once more went still as they attempted to see and hear what was happening.

After a murmured conversation the king glowered, then struck his fist into his other hand. The gasps around Hadassah confirmed what she had already guessed. Queen Vashti had refused to come!

Mordecai's foreboding expression was further proof to Hadassah of the dire situation. "What's going to happen to her?" she asked in a whisper. Mordecai just shook his head with a solemn look on his face.

After the buzz of questions and predictions had filled the hall, the king's second-in-command, Memucan, stepped to the front of the platform and there was immediate silence.

"Queen Vashti has refused to obey His Majesty's command, and a royal edict has been proclaimed," he said in a loud voice, "written in the law of Persia so that it cannot be changed, that Vashti's royal position is taken from her and will be given to another more worthy than she."

The hall nearly exploded in cries of dismay along with some shouts of glee. To the commoners at the court, this kind of announcement filled them with uncertainty and fear. The very fickle nature of the edict made them worry about the ominous consequences that might impact their own lives. For members of the royal court, the circle of men around the king, each one immediately began thinking about how he could use this event to further his own position and standing with the king.

If Mordecai and Hadassah had been closer to the king's dais, they might have seen the expressions of greed and opportunity flitting across the face of Haman as he lounged beside the king, watching him closely.

CHAPTER FIVE

HADASSAH LEANED ON THE WINDOWSILL, HOLDING her beautiful keepsake medallion up to catch the moonlight sifting through the trees in the courtyard. She had been absolutely stunned when Papa Mordecai had presented it to her after they had finished their evening meal, a special one in celebration of her special day. She had just turned eighteen, and he explained that he had kept it for her all these years since that dreadful day when she had celebrated an earlier birthday.

"Do you remember it?" Mordecai asked her as she held the necklace in her hands.

She couldn't even speak as her finger traced the star outline. *I didn't just imagine this,* she said to herself in awe. *It's real. . . .*

She finally looked up at him and nodded her head slowly. "Yes, yes, I do. I remember her placing it in my hands. . . . It must have been my mother. Her face is not very clear to me, but, yes, I recall that . . . it was my birthday, and I think I was turning seven." She stopped to stare at the pendant again. "I begged to wear it to bed."

"And you were wearing it when you came flying through the flames into my arms," Mordecai finished for her. He had placed his hand over hers on the table and smiled at her. "I am so glad you lived, Hadassah. You have brought such joy into my life. Thank you."

Hadassah had a lump in her throat, and her smile was a bit wobbly when she answered, "Thank you, too, Papa Mordecai, for giving me a home and love and for raising me as your own to love and honor God."

"I think you are old enough now to have this medallion. It was passed along from your great-great-grandmother, who brought it with her from Israel long ago."

Hadassah had nodded as Mordecai's words reminded her of the family story her parents had told her many years before.

"I know you will guard it carefully and wisely," he finished.

Hadassah told him she would do so. Then she grinned at Mordecai. "And 'keep it hidden from those who shouldn't know of my Jewish heritage,'" she said in a singsong tone, quoting his oft-stated warnings about secrecy to her. He nodded and smiled back, but his expression was very sober.

Hadassah knew his concerns came out of his deep love and care for her, and she was learning to respect the need for secrecy herself. She shivered as the face of Haman and the merchant's demolished stall came unbidden to her memory. She shook her head slightly and went on to another more recent memory.

Now she was thinking about last night's banquet and the king's new edict to replace Queen Vashti. The crowd had surged toward the platform, forcing Mordecai and Hadassah nearly to the bottom of the royal stairs. After Memucan, the King's Master of Audiences, had announced Vashti's banishment, he had gone on to say that the 127 provinces of Persia would be searched for the most beautiful maidens in the land from which King Xerxes would select his new queen.

While Hadassah had been watching Memucan's announcement, she noticed the king talking into the ear of one of the other men on the dais. Her heart nearly stopped beating when she recognized the man—it was Haman, the man she had seen in the market, the hater of Jews! There he was, listening intently to whatever the king was telling him.

Soon after, Haman had rushed down the steps and through the crowd only a short distance from where Hadassah and Mordecai were standing. Just as he hurried by, she saw an emblem on his tunic—that twisted cross again!

Hadassah had clung to Mordecai's arm, too terrified by the memories of the two terrible events connected with the emblem to say anything to him about it.

When Mordecai had returned from work that evening for her birthday supper, he had solemnly told them that

Queen Vashti indeed had been banished from the realm. Hadassah could only quake inwardly at the likelihood that Haman had been on his way from the banquet to carry out that very sentence. Hadassah imagined the poor woman being dragged to the Persian border and sent on her way into the desert—alone. Or worse. Hadassah shuddered and would not allow herself to imagine any further.

Instead, her thoughts went back to her own mother, and from her seat by the window she looked at the medallion again in the moonlight and tried to remember what her mother looked like. If she concentrated very hard, Hadassah thought she could see her face. Or was that her own face she was recalling? Hadassah felt sad that she couldn't be sure.

As Hadassah looked at the moon, she was not aware of someone gazing at her outside the walls across the courtyard, nor of the spear he held that also glinted in the moonlight like her medallion. She did not see him slip quietly away, an evil grin on his face, when she had risen from the window to go to bed.

The next morning Hadassah and Mordecai were awakened before dawn by frantic knocking on the door. He always bolted it at night after Rachel returned to her own home, and he stumbled out of bed to see who it was. Hadassah joined him, rubbing sleep from her eyes. When Mordecai opened the door, there stood Rachel, disheveled and wailing frantically.

"It's Jesse! They've taken Jesse!" she wept.

"What happened? Who's taken him?" Mordecai almost shouted in order to get Rachel to answer coherently.

"We don't know—he's been missing since yesterday afternoon," Rachel gasped out, her voice raw with emotion. "His parents have searched the streets. We . . . we have heard rumors of an army patrol taking away groups of young men. . . ."

Mordecai's groan made Rachel sink to her knees with her face in her hands, shaking and weeping like her heart would break. Hadassah felt as though her whole body had turned to stone.

"Yes," he finally said slowly, laying his hand on Rachel's trembling shoulder, "an edict went out from the palace yesterday that five hundred handsome young men were to be rounded up and taken to the citadel at the palace. They are to serve the king and help guard the young maidens being selected as a possible queen." He straightened up and looked back and forth between Hadassah and Rachel, shaking his head in deep sorrow. "I never thought they would take Jesse—"

"No-o-o-o-o," suddenly came in a long cry deep from within Hadassah. The terror that filled her being spurred her body into motion. She whirled around and was out the door before Mordecai could get to her.

CHAPTER SIX

HADASSAH'S LEGS CHURNED BENEATH HER AS SHE ran up the street toward the palace. Oh, she had to find Jesse! He was too young, too wonderful, too dear to her to be held against his will away from all who loved him, away from a normal life. She knew in her heart, which was pounding both from exertion and terror, that this meant Jesse was destined to be a lifelong member of the king's court, forced to do whatever the king wanted as long as he had breath, with no chance to marry or have a family of his own.

"Jesse! Jesse!" came with each gasp as Hadassah ran up to the palace gates. The guards crossed their spears firmly in front of the entrance as the distraught young woman, wearing only the tunic she had slept in, halted before them.

Hadassah tried to calm herself. "I'm looking for—do you know if—" But she stopped at the looks of derision on their faces. She turned away, weeping almost hysterically when she realized the hopelessness of it all. She slowly started back down the street toward home.

In the distance she saw Mordecai running toward her,

waving his arms wildly and shouting. She could not hear what he was saying over some commotion in the street behind her. As the clatter of noise grew louder, she turned to look over her shoulder—at a column of marching soldiers headed straight for her!

Hadassah quickly moved to the side and flattened herself against a wall. She was not particularly alarmed since columns of soldiers frequently moved through the streets at all hours of the day and night. Now she was able to hear Mordecai's shouts above the sounds of the marching feet, frantically calling her name as he ran.

In another moment Hadassah was surrounded by the soldiers. She backed up as far as she could against the wall, feeling the rough stone against her hands as she tried to make herself as small and insignificant as she could.

Her heart hammered in her chest as the leader of the soldiers stood in place and looked her up and down. "What have we here?" he asked in mock humor. Hadassah made herself look up into the face of the soldier who had planted himself in front of her. "This must be the one you were telling me about, Kasmir, that 'beautiful young lass' you saw the other night. She looks a bit disheveled right now, but I think she'll make a nice addition to the group of contestants. If she's dressed correctly, she just might be the next queen of Persia!" The other soldiers laughed loudly. Their rough comments chilled Hadassah to the bone.

Hadassah nearly wept in relief as she heard the wonderful sound of her father's voice. "What is going on here?" he demanded. But Hadassah could hear the tremor of fear in his voice.

"Oh, we're collecting beautiful young women—like this one here—to be presented to the king. He's looking for a new queen, you know—"

"But she is exempt! She is not to be included in the king's edict." By then Mordecai had pushed through the ring of soldiers and stood staring into Hadassah's frightened eyes.

"So you know this lovely maiden?" the soldier demanded. Mordecai, now speechless with sorrow, could only nod. "Well, scribe, I know who you are and where you live. You've got two days to get her ready for her trip to the palace. Make sure you do it. We will be at your door after two sundowns." He turned on his heel and the other soldiers followed him, jeering and laughing among themselves.

"Oh, my Hadassah," Mordecai whispered through trembling lips. "What will—what will we do? What will happen to you?" He knew that, just like Jesse, if she was taken into the palace, she might never be allowed to return home. And then they both were weeping in each other's arms. They stood in the street rocking back and forth.

"Hadassah, my love, we must return home," Mordecai finally said to her. "We do not have much time. We must think about what we can do. . . ." His voice trailed off as he

turned her around and led her down the street while she cried and clung to his arm.

Hadassah's fears for Jesse were now mingled with her own fears. She and Rachel spent most of the day crying and begging God to help all of them.

Mordecai did not go to work that day, and he spent those first hours in a corner of his bedroom rocking back and forth with his head bowed and his lips moving in prayer.

When he finally came out to them, he motioned for the two women to join him at the table. He reached for Hadassah's hand and held it tightly.

"I have asked the Lord for deliverance for you, Hadassah," he began, his voice full of emotion. "For you and for Jesse," he added with a glance at Rachel. "But I do not know what the Lord intends to do in this situation. What I have come to know over many years of praying and reading the sacred scrolls is that we cannot dictate what the Almighty must do."

He now reached for Rachel's hand. "I believe we must—" he paused to gain control of his voice— "we must plan for the worst and prepare for Hadassah to go to the palace." He cleared his throat and squeezed both of the hands, one smooth and soft, the other calloused and wrinkled, that he held. Renewed sobs from both women once more filled the room.

"We do not know at this time what God has in mind

for you, Hadassah," he continued over the sound of their weeping, "but I believe He has something planned that we don't understand right now. For Jesse, too. But we will at the right time. Remember when we talked about the 'why?' of life's tragedies after your parents were killed? We cannot foretell the future, but we can remain confident in God's love. Stay close to your God, my daughter," he encouraged, his voice stronger as the truth he was speaking entered his own sorrowful heart.

Those next two days were filled with more tears and sorrow, but as Mordecai continued to pray to God and talk with Hadassah about what was to come, she was able to take comfort in his words of instruction and the scriptures he read to her.

"Even more than ever, you must remember to keep your Jewishness a secret," he warned her over and over. "You do not know who is a friend and who might be the enemy around the palace," he said. And Hadassah saw the face of Haman flash before her. But she said nothing about her concerns to her poor father, who already was worried enough.

Mordecai thought of everything he could tell her about the palace and about conducting herself with the other candidates for queen.

"I cannot say at this time, my Hadassah," he said, "whether the Almighty's plan is for you to win the position of queen." He could not go on for a moment, and

Hadassah squeezed his hand, not knowing which of them needed the most comfort.

"But remember the scriptures you have learned," he finally continued, "the stories you have read about our people and our land. And every day I will meet you in the evening at the eastern gate of the palace. We can talk and pray together, and you can tell me everything I need to know. I will do the same for you. And in some way we know not at this time, God will bring deliverance. . . ."

Hadassah had myriad questions and things she wanted to talk over before it was too late, but her mind was nearly numb with her emotions and uncertainties.

The household barely slept at all, knowing their precious time together was nearly over.

"Maybe I should keep the medallion for you, Hadassah," Mordecai suggested in the early hours as the fateful morning drew near. "It could identify you." But Hadassah burst into a new flood of tears and begged to keep it with her.

"It's all I have of my family, of you," she cried. "I'll keep it hidden, safe, and no one will know what it is or where it came from," she promised through trembling lips to Mordecai's reluctant agreement.

CHAPTER SEVEN

HADASSAH WAS WEEPING SO HARD SHE COULD
hardly see Mordecai's beloved face as she said good-bye to
him, then to Rachel.

"I'll watch for any news of Jesse," she told Rachel as the
woman clung to her. "I'll try to get word to Papa about
whatever I can—"

Rachel's nearly hysterical sobs drowned out further conversation.

The soldiers grouped around the open doorway seemed
to realize the consequences of their grim task and quietly
moved back a step or two to give the three a bit of privacy
for the final parting.

After some final whispered words from Mordecai in her
ear, Hadassah took a deep breath, squared her shoulders,
and gave them each one more embrace. As the soldiers surrounded her and began the long, sad march up the street to
the palace, she could hear Mordecai's trembling voice in the
ancient words, "'Hear, O Israel: the Lord our God . . .'"
Hadassah strained to listen as long as she could until the

well-loved words were lost to the staccato sound of the soldiers' feet.

"'When I am afraid,'" she quoted under her breath, "'I will trust in you.'" She repeated the words from the Psalm until they were at the palace gates.

Hadassah stared up at the entrance through which she had walked with Mordecai to the banquet only days ago, but it seemed like a lifetime had passed since then. This time the gates shut behind her with a finality that sent a shudder through her body. Her knees felt weak and she nearly collapsed, but two soldiers grasped each arm firmly and steered her forward.

They came to the doors of a smaller citadel within the palace grounds, and a sharp order from one of the soldiers brought a tall man to the entrance. He looked down at Hadassah with something like sympathy in his eyes, and her quaking heart felt a glimmer of hope stir within her.

"I'll take her from here," he told the soldiers in an authoritative voice, and they melted away as the man escorted Hadassah into the hallway and closed the door behind her.

"I know all this is very frightening," he said in a soothing voice, "but I promise you will be fine."

He led Hadassah to a dark and cool room further inside the building. As her eyes adjusted to the dimness, she noticed several soft-looking velvet-covered pillows arrayed around the walls of the room.

"What is your name, my dear?" he asked.

"Hadas—" she began but then quickly stopped herself. It was a very Jewish name, meaning *myrtle,* and Mordecai's warnings echoed inside her head. She frantically searched her mind for another name she could give him. "Star," she finally said weakly, overwhelmed by the emotions that came with remembering the name her mother had given her along with the medallion.

"My name is Hegai," the tall man informed her. "I am also called the King's Chamberlain. I am in charge of all the young maidens who are being brought to the palace to contend for the title Queen of Persia." He looked more carefully at Hadassah, then said, "I was going to have you wait here in this anteroom for some of the others to arrive. But you look very tired, little one. I'm going to bring you to your sleeping chamber for a rest."

Again Hadassah nearly gave in to tears at the kind tone of his words. Hegai led her down another marble hallway, then into a high-ceilinged room lit from a window on a courtyard. He brought her over to a low platform covered with layers of sheepswool, and Hadassah sank down onto its softness.

"Here now, you get some rest," Hegai invited. Hadassah nodded numbly and put her head down on the bed. She had gotten very little sleep during the last few days, and even the lump in her throat and the tears burning behind her eyelids could not keep her from slumber.

Hadassah was awakened once or twice by sounds in the

hallway beyond the door—whimpering from young girls like her, then the deep, comforting voice of Hegai as he led them to rooms further down the hall. Hadassah's dreams were mixed with her recent memories of being separated from her beloved Papa Mordecai and Rachel. And where was Jesse? She wept again and slept once more.

When Hadassah awoke next, she was at first confused, then shocked. Nearly all her life she had slept in the same room and the same bed in Mordecai's house. Now her eyes opened to the sight of strange walls and ceiling, and she sat up with a gasp of fright.

Then realization of where she was and why came flooding back, and a sob caught in her throat. She took a deep breath to calm herself, then slowly stood and moved toward the window.

The light coming in from the courtyard was the kind that is difficult to distinguish between evening and morning, and Hadassah was not sure how long she had been sleeping. She stood on tiptoe and craned her neck to see over the edge of the high window. She saw western sunlight bathing the trees and flowers of the garden in afternoon glow. But the morning's events seemed far longer ago than this very day.

Maybe I could escape! raced through her mind as she examined a nearby cherry tree brushing at the edges of the window, with a marble terrace and a pool at its far edge. But on further thought, Hadassah quickly remembered that every gate in the high outer wall of the palace was under heavy guard. There was no way she would be able to sneak by them.

Am I a prisoner? was her next thought. She looked away from the beautiful garden outside the window to the lovely furnishings of the room, and her surroundings didn't seem anything like a prison. She walked over to the door and silently pushed it open to the marble hallway opening on to another garden courtyard with more trees and a smaller pool.

The beauty of it all touched Hadassah's soul, and her heart began to lift from the heaviness that had nearly overwhelmed her upon awakening in this strange but stunning place.

Then she remembered Papa Mordecai's final whispered instructions to her that morning. *Meet me at the East Gate!* She knew what she had to do next.

Hadassah hurried back to the bedchamber and stared once more at the high window. She would need something to stand on, she decided. Quickly looking around, she saw a low footstool she was sure would get her up on the windowsill. Soon she was balancing on the narrow edge, grasping branches of the cherry tree, then sliding down the outer wall to the ground.

She stood very still and carefully looked around to see if anyone was watching her. Seeing no one, she tiptoed out from under the cherry tree and moved silently into the court-yard. Gauging the location of the sun, she began moving in the opposite direction, hopefully toward that eastern gate of the palace Mordecai had mentioned.

Hadassah stayed near the courtyard walls until she reached a small gate. Thankfully it pushed open at her touch, and she moved into another garden of trees and shrubs. She walked from tree to tree, stopping each time to look around for unwanted eyes observing her. So far she had seen no one.

At the next gateway she saw in the distance a group of young men sitting together on the ground under the trees. They seemed to be listening to a large Persian man who was standing in front of them and lecturing them about something.

Hadassah's heart felt like it had stopped when she sud-denly realized what she was seeing. These were the young men who were being rounded up to serve at the palace dur-ing the selection of the new queen!

Jesse is probably there! flashed through her mind, and her legs felt so weak they barely held her upright. She slowly moved back, away from the gate, to a nearby tree where she could watch the group without being seen. Straining, she all of a sudden caught sight of the familiar face. *Jesse!* She breathed his name under her breath. She wondered if he had glanced her way, but she couldn't be sure.

She must move on, she finally decided, before someone else did see her. Her heart thudded in her chest as she continued her journey toward the eastern gate.

She finally found herself at the high outer wall, and she paused again to determine which way she should go. Looking once more at the sun's descent in the western sky, she decided to turn right. Up ahead the wall was broken by a thick column and a wide gap defined by a large gate made of iron bars. Hadassah sighed in relief. The East Gate.

She tiptoed up to the edge of the column and looked around it through the bars. She saw no soldiers, only merchants going about their business. She moved closer to press her face against the bars. And there was Papa Mordecai.

He looked worn and tired, no doubt having stood vigil there since Hadassah had been taken that morning. The two grasped hands through the bars, both of them weeping so hard Mordecai could barely get the words out: "Hadassah, my dearest, are you all right?"

She could not reply but simply kissed the tips of his fingers grasping hers. Her emotions were a mixture of deep sadness at their separation and joy at the sight of him again. She felt as if she had not seen him for years instead of barely one day.

"Oh, Papa Mordecai," Hadassah finally was able to gasp out, "yes, I am all right." She felt his relief in his gentle squeeze of her hands. "Hegai, the chamberlain, is as you told me he would be, a very nice man," she continued, "and my quarters are comfortable. I was even able to sleep for a while," she added, trying to sound cheerful.

"Have you met any of the other girls, Hadassah?" he asked.

"None of them yet, Papa. I think I heard some of them arriving, but I have not seen anyone else since Hegai showed me to my sleeping chamber." She stared into the familiar face through the bars, then burst out with more tears. "Is there no way to get me out of here—home with you and Rachel again? You are a royal scribe and—"

But he was sorrowfully shaking his head, tears of his own coursing down his face. "I've already been making inquiries, Hadassah. This is a royal edict, and there is no way out of it without certain death—to both of us and probably Rachel and others in our Jewish community. No, there is nothing we can do but bear this fate as worthy children of Israel."

The sob in Hadassah's throat felt like it would choke her, but as she looked into her father's face, she realized she must be brave or they both would come completely undone with grief. She took a deep breath and nodded her acceptance of his words.

"Do you remember the things I told you?" Mordecai asked after his own deep breath. "You must, above all, love and obey God, and at the same time you must keep your Hebrew ancestry a secret. Promise me you'll follow these instructions as though your life depends on it. Because you know it does." He looked steadily into Hadassah's eyes as he waited for her answer.

"Yes, Papa, yes, I promise." Hadassah lowered her voice and looked around quickly to make sure they were not overheard. "Actually, I have already done something to protect the secret. When Hegai asked for my name, I told him my name was Star. I am keeping my medallion well hidden so no one knows of my Jewishness."

Mordecai nodded wistfully. "That was a wise decision, my dear. I should have thought of it myself." He looked about, too, then said, "Go, my precious one. And let's meet here each day. Early morning at dawn is best, but if for some reason either of us is not able to keep that time, the same place in the evening just as the sun touches the horizon."

Weeping again, the two leaned to kiss each other through the bars. As Mordecai slowly walked away, Hadassah could hear him praying for her. As she turned for the return trip to her quarters, she could barely see her way through her tears. "'When I am afraid, I will trust in you'" was her whispered chant until she climbed into the cherry tree and once more slid over the windowsill into her room.

CHAPTER EIGHT

SOON AFTER HADASSAH RETURNED TO THE BEDROOM, Hegai knocked on the door and entered. "You are looking more rested, Star," he announced. He looked down at her dusty feet. "Have you been out for a walk?" When Hadassah did not immediately reply, he went on, "Well, you no doubt are hungry by now. I will have some food brought to you. A nice roast of pork, some venison, some wine will do you worlds of good."

Hadassah gathered her courage and asked, "Please, may I ask that I be served only some bread and some fruit? And no pork." At his curious look, she hurried on, "I prefer lighter fare, and others of the girls may wish to join me in dishes that actually will improve our health, even our beauty. And water to drink will be fine."

He raised his eyebrows and nodded with a knowing smile. "Your request is granted, my dear."

Does he know I am Jewish? flashed through Hadassah's mind as Hegai bowed and went out the door. But if he did, Hadassah somehow knew the secret was safe with him. She felt the medallion under her tunic and decided she would need to find a safe place to hide it from any prying eyes.

Soon a young Persian servant girl entered the room with a tray of food just as Hadassah had requested. Though emotionally and physically at the end of her endurance, she was surprised to find herself hungry, and she began eating the fresh grapes, pomegranate seeds, and bread. Refreshed by the food and water and weary from the exhausting day, she soon lay back on her bed, said her prayers, and fell into a deep sleep.

The next morning Hadassah awoke with the dawn, made her trip to the East Gate—a journey that seemed much shorter now that she knew the way—and met with Mordecai. They both were very relieved to see the other looking rested and more accepting of their new situation.

"Rachel sends her love," Mordecai told Hadassah, who then remembered her glimpse of Jesse last evening. She quickly told her father about it, and he was very happy for this tiny piece of news to bring back to Rachel. The fact that Jesse was alive would do his family a world of good, even though they, too, were grieving the tragedy of separation.

After Hadassah was back in her room and had break-fasted on more fruit, Hegai gathered her along with the others who already had been collected as queen candidates and met with them in the courtyard.

He stood near the pool to address them, and his almost grandfatherly expression helped to put them somewhat at ease. "Young women," he began, "I am imagining that each of you is experiencing a wide array of emotions right now. Fear. Homesickness. Uncertainty. Loneliness. Along with anticipation, maybe even joy at being chosen for this contest. You are part of a highly select group, the most beautiful young women from the whole Persian empire." He paused to look around at the lovely faces arrayed before him. "Every one of you has a chance to become the queen of that whole empire." Some nervous tittering greeted his words as the group looked at each other, eyes wide and expressions a mix of delight and doubt.

"During the next year," he went on after they had turned again to him, "you will be provided with wonderful accommodations for your beauty sleep, the finest foods Persia can offer"—his eyes flickered briefly to Hadassah's, and she gave the tiniest of nods in acknowledgment of his consent to her request—"rare cosmetics from India, Lebanon, and Egypt to enhance your natural beauty, and lovely scents of myrrh and other spices from around the world."

Now the murmur of voices was louder, excitement overtaking their fears. Hegai raised his voice to get their attention. "At the end of this year of preparation, you each may select as much jewelry as you wish, any gown you choose, for your presentation to the king. Even if he does not choose you to be his queen, you may keep the clothing and jewels as your own."

This announcement evoked only silence as each girl contemplated her future and the enormously significant question: *Will I be the one chosen to be the next Queen of Persia, wife of King Xerxes?*

Hadassah sat quietly, thinking about that question and whether she even wanted to be queen. *Why am I here in this place, at this time?* she wondered. She did not know the answer, but somehow not knowing did not frighten her. She was gradually discovering that her trust in God was replacing the fear that had held her tightly in its grasp during the recent days.

As each new group of girls joined the candidates, Hegai gave them his same little speech. The young women—now some of them from as far away as India to the east and Macedonia in the west—settled into life in the palace and their preparations for the royal contest. Some had lighter hair and fair complexions, others were dark beauties with shiny black hair. With various personalities, interests, and family backgrounds, there was more than an occasional disagreement, and even some brawls, with many of the young women vying for the best chance of being selected as queen.

Hadassah was able to keep herself out of most of the disagreements, and she tried to be kind and considerate with each of the girls. They couldn't figure out how she kept herself slender while many of them were adding extra weight after eating all the rich foods. Hadassah encouraged those who would listen to eat more simply and only modest amounts as she was doing. When jealousy and bickering erupted into arguments, she tried to be a peacemaker and help each girl to understand the other's point of view. She was not always successful, but gradually the candidates began looking to her for advice and leadership during this time of preparation and waiting. A few of them even became friends with Hadassah, and some of her loneliness was lessened.

But there still were times when thoughts of her home and family, of Jesse and his friendship, nearly overwhelmed her with grief and loss. Those precious but fleeting moments with Mordecai through the bars of the eastern gate each day were not nearly enough to satisfy her longings or make her feel at home in her new surroundings. Even in the palace, surrounded by luxury and any material desire she could imagine, with maids waiting to serve her every need, Hadassah turned daily to God for comfort and strength and direction for her future.

Hadassah, along with the other candidates, settled into a rather predictable daily routine. Only an occasional fleeting glimpse of that twisted-cross emblem on the side of a distant warhorse or on a soldier's tunic jolted her from the quiet of her usual activities. She pushed from her mind the memories of the very first time she had seen the sign and the horror that accompanied that sight and concentrated on being the very best candidate she could.

ॐ

"I am coming to believe, Hadassah," began Mordecai

during one of their morning meetings, "that your being captured and brought to the palace was not simply a terrible accident. As I have been praying, it has come to me that our Lord has a divine purpose, one that we might not understand yet."

Hadassah stared intently into her father's eyes, seeing the depths of his love for God and for her as he talked.

"Remember when you were much younger and we discussed the 'why' of your parents' terrible death? I have no other answers for you than I had then. But I am thinking," he continued thoughtfully, "that you should set your mind toward being the very best candidate you can be."

Hadassah quickly nodded her agreement. "Yes, Papa, that is the very thought that has been coming to me, too. It may even be that—I hardly dare say it, and only to you—that I will be chosen to be the queen." Her voice dropped to nearly a whisper at the thought of it—to be selected above all the hundreds of beautiful maidens surrounding her was an incredible idea.

Mordecai was nodding his head slowly. "I had other plans for you, my little one," he said softly, "and I pictured you with a nice Jewish boy. . . ." Hadassah's mental image of Jesse, she was sure, was reflected in Mordecai's expression.

"But our Lord may indeed have another plan, one with implications we cannot even imagine," he said, once more reaching for her hands through the bars. "If you are to be the next queen, you must apply yourself in ways that go beyond

physical beauty—to educating your mind, training your emotions, and developing godly character. I am going to copy our
scriptures onto pieces of parchment so you can continue your
study of God's Word and the history of our people."

Hadassah's heart surged with joy at the thought of this
opportunity to once again read, to saturate her soul with
the truths of their Jewish history. To immerse her mind in
the accounts of God's interactions with her people gave her
an inner thrill, and she could scarcely contain her delight.

And so several times each week, Mordecai brought
Hadassah a carefully copied section of the Pentateuch, the
five books of Moses. He chose selections from each book in
order to give her the broadest knowledge of God's instructions to His people.

At the same time, Hadassah asked Hegai if one of the
maids could bring her volumes from the royal library. She
already knew how to speak Persian, but now she asked him
to teach her to read it. At first he was mystified by the
whole notion of a female even being interested in reading.

"I want to prepare myself in every way that I can," she
explained to his question, "to be a worthy candidate.
Besides physical beauty, I desire that my mind is also
attractive to the king."

Hegai looked at her for a long moment, then slowly nodded his agreement. After the scroll had arrived, he bent over
the parchment to point out the meaning of each mark
inscribed on it. He was amazed when after only a short time

Hadassah was able to read back to him from the scroll.

"'And the number of goats killed and prepared for the banquet was thirteen,'" she read to Hegai. Hadassah wrinkled her nose and looked up at the chamberlain. "Do you think there might be more interesting texts that I could read?" she asked.

Hegai laughed and told her he personally would select one. "Maybe something about King Xerxes' father, King Darius," he suggested.

"Yes, yes," Hadassah agreed enthusiastically, "that sounds most interesting. And the more I know about the king and his family . . ." Her voice drifted off, and Hegai patted her shoulder approvingly.

"You have come upon a most unusual strategy," he commended her, "and one that is likely to get the attention of the king. I will help you in any way I can."

And thus along with the ritual baths and daily massages with perfumed oils, Hadassah began regular meetings with Hegai, where he continued to teach her to read Persian as well as the protocols of the palace. She asked questions about the king. What were his likes and dislikes? Was there a particular scent he liked better than another? What of his family? Did he have any brothers or sisters? And on and on.

Hadassah's wealth of information about the king grew weekly, and Hegai's admiration for Hadassah grew along with it.

CHAPTER NINE

THE CHATTERING CROWD OF YOUNG WOMEN MOVED across the courtyard like an oversized flock of geese, with Hegai grimly in the lead. After tracing a path beyond the outer perimeters of the candidates' quarters, he brought the group up to a broad, low-slung building ringed by soldiers, spears at the ready. Two of them stepped forward and demanded Hegai's orders, which he promptly presented to them. One of them read the parchment carefully, nodded to his companion, then turned to begin the long process of sliding back the bars and removing the locks on the massive wooden door.

Hadassah, as curious as any of them, pressed forward with the others to catch the first glimpse of what lay behind the doors. But Hegai impatiently motioned them all back with a signal from his arm. Hadassah could tell he was not enjoying this particular expedition.

Slowly the heavy doors moved open, and the group strained to see into the near darkness. One of the guards lit a torch and passed it to Hegai. He stepped into the gloom, and the place blazed into light.

It took a few moments for the women's eyes to adjust to the change, and then a collective gasp echoed into the room from the doorway. As far as it could reach, the torch's glow reflected back from countless gold pieces—jewelry of earrings and necklaces, goblets, plates of all kinds and sizes, daggers, swords, and on and on. Hadassah put a hand over her eyes to protect them from the glittering brilliance.

Shrieking, three girls launched themselves into the room, scrambling for jeweled tiaras hanging just out of reach.

"Stop immediately!" shouted Hegai. Hadassah was startled at his tone, having never heard him raise his voice before. "You will conduct yourselves with dignity in the king's treasury," he instructed sternly. "This is where the Crown stores the bounty of many battles—fortune from Babylon, gold from Egypt, wealth from Phoenicia and countries you've never even heard of." He paused to sweep the group with his gaze.

"Today you are invited to select any items you would like to wear for your presentation to the king," he told them. "You may take as much as you can wear from this chamber, and it will be yours for the keeping, whether or not you are chosen to be queen."

Hadassah could feel the stirring around her as the girls set themselves to plunge after their gold fortunes. At another motion of Hegai's arm, they rushed inside, clawing through the displays of jewelry with shouts of delight or anger, depending on whether they had gotten to their selections in time.

Hadassah held back, then slowly moved into the room and between the rows of stolen riches from so many conquered nations—no doubt including the nation of Israel. She let her eyes drift across the staggering array of wealth, but unlike the others, she could feel no urge to decorate herself with the relics of nations and peoples crushed into defeat and now dominated by Persia.

She paused by a display of necklaces, and her hand drifted over the various pieces hanging by their chains. Then her heart nearly stopped as she touched a medallion—and its six-pointed star!

"What have you found, Star?" asked a deep voice over her shoulder. Hadassah swiftly turned, her panic subsiding when she saw it was Hegai. Numbly she held out the medallion to him.

"I see you have discovered a very interesting piece of jewelry," he commented, reaching out his hand to accept it from her. He turned it over several times, then asked, "Do you know which country this came from?"

Hadassah's heart nearly stopped again as she frantically

tried to think of how to answer him. She did not want to lie, and yet—

"I believe it comes from a country east of here," Hegai interrupted her thoughts, saving her from having to answer. "Hmmm, it is a Hebrew piece," he went on as he examined it closely. "See, it has the six-pointed star, symbol of the nation of Israel." Hegai lifted his eyes to examine her face as carefully as he had the medallion.

Hadassah only nodded, finally dropping her eyes as her cheeks burned. *What does Hegai know about me?* she silently asked herself again. But then the man had moved over to another display and was asking her if any of them interested her.

Relieved at the change of subject, Hadassah asked him, "Which one do you think the king would like?" Hegai did not answer but simply stood there with the faintest hint of a smile on his face and shaking his head slightly.

Hadassah was becoming concerned that maybe she had offended him or breached some unknown royal protocol that prohibited such a question. "Master Hegai, did I say something wrong or—"

"No, no, little Star, nothing like that." He quickly assured her. "Far from it. You see, this is the very first time any candidate has ever asked me a question like that. To care about the king and his desires, his preferences, is a most unusual trait." He stood looking at her another long moment, then said, "I have decided to give you a place of leadership among the other girls, and I will exhort them to follow your example. I am sure you are able to take on this task, are you not, Star?"

She could only nod dumbly. But Hegai was not finished. He lifted her hand, turned it over, and placed the six-pointed star medallion into it. "This is the one for you, my dear, and I'm sure the king will appreciate it, too." He folded her fingers around it, then waved his arm around the glowing room. "But there is much more here for you to select from. Please, look for other things to take with you— whether or not you make use of them at your presentation to the king."

Hegai smiled and moved away, but Hadassah felt like she had become rooted to the floor. She glanced once more at the medallion, then tucked it away inside her tunic. What did it all mean? The chamberlain's special gift to her, along with the most interesting conversation with him, then to be appointed First Candidate over the other girls. . . . She felt like she had received a special blessing, and she whispered a prayer of thanks.

As it turned out, Hadassah did wander farther among the piles of gold, but she left the treasury with only the medallion that seemed like a twin to her own.

❧

Hadassah was returning from her usual morning visit

with Mordecai, and she passed the gate over which she had spotted Jesse during her first days at the palace. She always glanced that way just in case the group of young men might be there again, but she had never seen anyone there since that first time. Until now.

She stopped as still as a statue. Under one of the fruit trees across the wall, she could see Jesse standing underneath, holding a basket of oranges. He was looking up into the tree and talking to someone.

Hadassah did not move a muscle and just stood watching him while her heart thudded in her chest. It felt like she stood there for hours, but eventually another young man slid down from the tree with a sack full of more oranges. He dumped them into Jesse's basket and then the two had some discussion. Jesse handed the full basket to his companion, who moved off quickly and was soon out of sight.

Jesse turned back toward the tree, but suddenly his head swung around and he looked directly at Hadassah. He, too, stood as if rooted to the spot, and then he looked quickly about and moved toward her almost at a run.

"Oh, Jesse . . ." Hadassah whispered as she reached to him across the gate. As their hands met, she blurted out, "You look the same—I mean, it seems like I haven't seen you for years, but I . . . I would have recognized you anywhere." She realized she was stammering with nervousness and excitement, and her cheeks felt warm with embarrassment.

"Hello, Hadassah," Jesse said, his voice holding both tenderness and sorrow. "I did not know for a long time you were here at the palace, but Hegai must have guessed that I am a Jew. He drew me aside one day and asked if I might know a beautiful young Jewess who called herself Star. When he described you further, I was sure it was you. I was very glad to hear something about you after all this time, but I am so sorry you are a candidate. I had other plans. . . ."

His voice faltered, and Hadassah squeezed his hand.

"Here, Jesse." She motioned toward a nearby tree that hung over the wall. "Let's move over here where we are less likely to be seen." Jesse grasped the top of the wall with both hands and launched himself over to Hadassah's side as she gasped in delight and fear—thrilled to see him again and fully aware of the risk to both of them if they were discovered.

"Yes, Jesse," Hadassah said as they moved under the protection of the tree branches and a thick bush growing next to the wall, "I had other plans, too." She dropped her eyes, and her cheeks once more grew warm. When she lifted her eyes to his, he was shaking his head mournfully.

"Oh, Hadassah," he said softly several times. Then his expression changed. "They have taken even my name away from me," he said, bitterness coloring his tone. "I am now

Hathach, not Jesse. I will never see my family again, and I will never have a normal life—"

"Shhhh," Hadassah whispered, touching a finger to his lips. "My name is gone, too. I am now Star, as Hegai told you. I gave him that name instead of Hadassah when I came here in order to help conceal my identity. Mordecai warned me through the years that the same evil marauders who killed my parents could still be a threat to me if they knew I had survived and might point the finger at them. And, Jesse"—here Hadassah dropped her voice even lower—"I have seen more than once an emblem I saw on a tunic that night." A shiver went through her body at the memory. "I cannot be sure, of course, but the soldiers I have seen wearing it are evil, and their leader is a wicked man who hates Jews."

Jesse grasped her shoulders and looked into her face. "What does the emblem look like?"

"It's like two lines crossing, like this"—she picked up a stick and drew in the sand—"with a short line at the four ends, like this." Hadassah completed the diagram and stood upright. "I call it a twisted cross."

Jesse stared at it a long time. "Yes," he said slowly. "I, too, have seen such a symbol. I will watch and take note of where I see it and who is wearing it. I will find a way to warn you if I hear anything of concern."

Hadassah told Jesse that she met with Mordecai every morning, and she would tell him about this visit with Jesse.

"Please send greetings and my love to my family, but please be careful, Hadassah. Besides getting in trouble ourselves, Mordecai and Grandmother Rachel and others in our families could be captured and dragged before the king. Who knows what punishment—"

"I promise to be extremely careful," Hadassah said quickly. "Hegai likes me and has given me a position of First Candidate over the others, and I have the impression he is watching out for me."

Jesse put his face into his hands and groaned. "'First Candidate . . .'" he repeated. "That means Hegai thinks you have a very good chance of being chosen queen." The sorrow in his voice made tears come to Hadassah's eyes.

"I have been talking to Papa Mordecai about this, Jesse," she was finally able to say, "and we are coming to believe that it's possible God has allowed all this to happen for a purpose. Maybe I am destined to be selected as the next Queen of Persia for some special reason—maybe to protect our people from some unknown harassment—or worse."

Jesse lifted his head, and Hadassah could see tears in his eyes, too. Then he shook his head again and tried to laugh. "My little Hadassah—Queen of Persia! Wouldn't that be something?"

As she returned to her room after their farewell, Hadassah took a bit of hope from Jesse's last comment. Maybe eventually he would be able to accept the reality of their situation and would trust the Lord with the future as she was learning to do. But most of all she hoped they could remain friends.

When she told Mordecai about the chance meeting with Jesse, he, too, was delighted with more news for Rachel, though he took the opportunity to caution Hadassah once more about the precariousness of her position and the risk of such meetings.

"I do realize it, Papa, and I will be very, very careful. And besides, I wouldn't want to do anything that would cause danger for Jesse. I could never forgive myself if he were to be punished because of something I caused."

Mordecai nodded soberly. But despite his own cautions to her, the next time he and Hadassah met for their morning rendezvous, he was carrying a small bag of things for Jesse from his grandmother Rachel.

"Just a few fig-filled pastries and some items of clothing," he explained quickly, "nothing that could be identified if a guard were to question you about it."

Now that Hadassah and Jesse knew a place where they could talk unseen by curious eyes, they began to meet rather regularly, concealed behind the bush and the wall surrounding the candidates' area.

Occasionally several of the young men were escorted

into the maidens' courtyard to do some required repairs or gardening or other duties. If one of them turned out to be Jesse, Hadassah carefully avoided eye contact with him in case even that small connection would somehow give away their friendship and the secret of their Hebrew heritage.

CHAPTER TEN

THE CANDIDATES WERE NOW IN THE SECOND HALF
of the year-long preparations for their presentations to the
king. This meant that minor spats even more easily turned
into jealous rages as the girls fought for the best of spices
and oils and cosmetics in order to ensure winning the
attention of the king. Hadassah often felt discouraged and
even angry as the bickering and quarreling grew in intensity.

As First Candidate, Hadassah prayed for grace and wisdom to be a good example to the rest of them and to be a
peacemaker among them when tensions got the best of
them. She invited various girls to share the specially
selected spices Hegai provided to her, and she helped them
experiment with various ways of applying cosmetics such as
Egyptian kohl to darken their eyes, blush on cheeks with
mulberry juice, and lips made rosy with flecks of iron oxide.
Each girl was striving to be the most attractive and appealing she possibly could be.

Hadassah acknowledged to herself that she had the
same goal. "But, God," she prayed, "keep my heart pure,

and help me to keep the real goal always before me—to be ready to do your bidding at a moment's notice."

One afternoon when Jesse met Hadassah, he looked rather despondent. Hadassah immediately asked him if something was wrong. He didn't answer her right away, but finally he said that, yes, something was very wrong.

He slid down the wall, his back to it, until he was sitting on the ground behind the bush. Hadassah quickly joined him, very concerned.

"There is a conspiracy going on in the palace, Hadassah, and one of the candidates is part of it. One of my friends was taking a rest up in a tree after dark last night, and he overheard a man talking to one of your competitors. He called her Misgath."

Hadassah immediately pictured the girl, a rather dour person with a superior attitude who mostly kept to herself.

"He threatened this Misgath," Jesse continued, "and gave her a bottle of some kind of mild poison with which she is to contaminate the food of every leading candidate before her presentation to the king. Not to kill her, but you can imagine a girl's chances if she's throwing up—"

But Hadassah frantically motioned for him to stop and said, "Yes, yes, I understand. But can't I just tell Hegai? He will believe me, I'm sure, and Misgath will be dealt with."

"I'm afraid not, Hadassah. Misgath is the daughter of one of the king's royal council, and probably even Hegai would be punished or even killed if he brought up such charges against this girl."

Jesse looked away for a moment, then turned back to Hadassah and said, "There's more. Misgath was instructed to find out if any of the candidates are Jewish, and she is to bring that information to this man."

"Who is he?" demanded Hadassah. "Maybe he can be exposed."

"My friend did not recognize him," Jesse answered. "The only thing he could make out was a tattoo on his arm, very prominent against the man's dark skin. Hadassah, what my friend described to me sounds just like that emblem you told me about—"

"The twisted cross!" the two said in unison.

Hadassah felt her body go cold and she struggled to breathe. When she finally could speak again, she asked, "What should I do?"

Jesse looked into her face for a long moment, then said, "Win. Win the king's favor and become Queen of Persia. That is our only hope—for you, for your family and mine, for the Jews of Persia."

As Hadassah crept back to her room, she felt an enormous weight of responsibility on her shoulders. "Oh, God," she prayed, "I cannot do this on my own. Please give me confidence and peace as I go forward. And if it is your will, give me favor with the king. . . ."

As the twelve months of training for the candidates was nearing its end, the continual topic of conversation among them was who would be first to be introduced to the king and how that candidate would be selected. And what if the king chose the first one he saw for his queen? They all knew that the future for the rest of them was rather bleak—on the one hand very secure, with everything they wanted or needed, except for a normal life. Those who were not chosen to be queen would live in the palace for the rest of their lives, ladies-in-waiting for the royal household. But they would never marry or have families of their own. The desperate longing in every girl's heart was that she would be the one who would strike King Xerxes' fancy to be the next Queen of Persia.

The last weeks were filled with frantic scrambling to lose any extra weight, to determine the perfect cosmetics and hairstyle, to try on and reject and try on again the right gowns and tunics for the occasion, and to choose what jewelry would accompany them on the fateful appearance before the king.

Hadassah chose not to join the candidates for one last visit to the royal treasury, but she heard about it from Jesse, who had been one of the guards on this final excursion. He chuckled as he described the mad dash into the piles and racks of jewelry and gold hair ornaments, the near stampede for one particularly ornate gold chain.

Hadassah had a different plan, though. Her many conversations with Hegai had brought her to the decision to wear a simple gown and only one piece of jewelry. Further, she intended to leave that one adornment with the king—so he would be reminded of her and of her name. . . .

Hegai assembled the candidates for one more meeting in the courtyard of their quarters. The usual chatter and banter was replaced by a tense silence as each girl searched his face for any sign of what was to come. Did his glance linger on one of them any longer than the other?

Hegai held up his hand and announced, "As you know, we have come to the time to begin the final contest. Using a method that only I will know, we will begin, one by one, to introduce you to the king. It may be that he will wish to see all of you before he makes his choice, or it could happen that just the right candidate will be identified and selected before he has interviewed every last one of you."

At the uncomfortable stirring among the young women, Hegai said, "You will all need to be patient and cooperative during this time. I will be watching and determining who should go next." At this the girls all became utterly still and composed their faces into as winsome an expression as they could manage.

Watching the group from her place at the end of the front row, Hadassah could hardly hide her smile at their rather childish ways. From all she had learned from Hegai, it would take more than a coy look to get the king's attention.

At the end of the meeting, the chamberlain had not identified which one would be first for an audience with the king, but not long afterward the news circled among them like wildfire: It was to be the daughter of the governor of Babylon, a young woman named Olandra. Hadassah couldn't help but feel sorry for her as the poor thing went from exhilaration one moment to abject terror the next.

Later that day, news of Olandra's encounter with the king traveled around the candidates' quarters with more speed than the news of her being the first. She had selected a most lavish gown, had thickly slathered on the cosmetics, and lacquered her hair into an ornate sculpture ornamented with every jeweled hair comb it could hold. With great difficulty she had tottered up to the doorway of the king's chambers, and then the very worst imaginable had occurred: She had become violently ill, right in front of the king. Obviously he had not been impressed, and the unfortunate girl was quickly ushered away to her new home away from the candidates and among the royal ladies-in-waiting.

"She must have gotten so nervous that her stomach couldn't hold her last meal" was the conclusion of the other girls. All except Misgath. Hadassah watched the girl, lurking on the edges of the gossiping crowd and looking furtively around. But no one else seemed to notice her.

Hadassah's heart thudded with the knowledge of the

poison conspiracy, and she wondered again if there was anything she could do to head off any further disasters as the candidates prepared for their appointments with the king. But she went over in her mind that last conversation with Jesse, and she couldn't think of anything else except to be watchful and vigilant herself.

CHAPTER ELEVEN

WITHIN DAYS—THOUGH IT SEEMED MUCH LONGER—
Hegai came to Hadassah with the news that it was her turn
to be presented to the king. Her emotions immediately
began jumping back and forth between fear and anticipation, and she begged him to tell her if she was truly ready.

He smiled down at her, laid a hand on her shoulder,
and answered, "Yes, my little Star, you are shining brightly
enough to catch the king's eye—and he has seen enough
beautiful women across the empire to recognize one who
has true beauty." Hegai lifted her chin to look her directly
in the eye and said, "He will see the inner loveliness of
mind and heart that make you so special, Star."

In spite of Hegai's encouragement, Hadassah's mind
swirled with questions and fears as she carefully began the
final preparations. She had already selected her gown, a
simple pale blue silk, and Hegai was in complete agreement, nodding his approval when she showed it to him. As
she bathed in sweet-smelling myrrh, she wondered once
more if she would be beautiful enough. Putting on the
gown and smoothing its folds around her, she silently asked

herself if the king would find her interesting and attractive, more so than the other candidates whom he had already seen.

Going over to her bed, Hadassah reached far underneath to a storage basket holding her
clothing and
personal items.
Underneath
everything else
she found a
small wooden
box, and she
quickly lifted it
out. She held it
in her hands, then
slowly opened the

the lid. Shining up at her from inside were two medallions, nearly identical six-pointed stars on gold chains. But she knew which one was the family heirloom. She carefully raised it and touched it to her lips before returning it to the box. This irreplaceable gift from her parents and from Mordecai would never leave her possession, she told herself once more.

But she picked up the other one and placed it around her neck. Just then a knock on the door signaled the entrance of a maid with a tray of food, followed by—Misgath! "Here, my lady," said the maid, "is some food for you. Misgath herself selected just the things you like—some fruit and—"

"No, I am not hungry," Hadassah interrupted.

"But you *must* eat," Misgath put in, her tone very soothing. "You will need your strength to be your best on this important day!" She was doing her best to be convincing, but Hadassah simply stood there shaking her head.

"I will eat later, Misgath, not now."

"But Hegai said that you were to be brought a tray, and—"

The door was flung open, and Jesse stood framed in the opening.

"Where did this food come from?" he demanded sharply.

"From the kitchen," the maid said timidly. "Misgath—"

In two steps Jesse had entered the room and snatched the tray from the trembling hands of the maid. "If the First Candidate does not wish to eat it, I will."

"No, no, it is for Star. Only she can—"

But Jesse already was eating the grapes and gulping the contents of the goblet. He turned to face Misgath.

"You are going to come with me to Hegai," he announced firmly. "When I become ill, you are going to tell him who gave you the poison I just drank. Your time as candidate will be over."

"Who are you to speak to me this way, Hathach? You

are a mere servant," she sneered. But Hadassah thought she could hear a thread of fear in her voice.

"I am charged with serving and protecting the candidates, Misgath," Jesse said as he doubled over with a groan of pain. "I don't think Hegai will lack for evidence of your treachery." Still clutching his stomach, he grabbed Misgath by the arm and dragged her from the room.

When she was again alone, Hadassah took a deep breath to quiet her heart, bowed her head, and prayed, "My Father in Heaven, may your will be done today. I have done everything in my power to be ready for whatever is ahead, and now I ask that you will be with me. . . ." Hadassah could say no more and tears flooded her eyes, but as she lifted her head and turned toward the door, an unexplained peace filled her heart. She squared her shoulders and moved determinedly toward whatever her future was going to be.

She paused a moment at the door, remembering yesterday morning when she and Mordecai had met at the gate for their traditional time together. They both knew it might be their last one before her audience with the king.

"I have set out to train my mind to be alert, my body to be healthy, and my appearance to be as attractive as it can be to win the favor of the king," she had whispered to Mordecai through the bars of the gate.

"Yes, my daughter, yes," Mordecai had agreed. "You have prepared yourself in every way over these last twelve months in order that he may select you. You will have a position of influence and power if you are the next queen, and maybe you will be able to protect your people from those who hate and kill Jews. . . ." He couldn't say any more, and Hadassah reached out to brush the tears from his eyes.

"I am ready, Papa," Hadassah had promised.

But have I done everything possible? She couldn't help but ask herself again as she now stood ready to leave her room. No, she would not allow herself any more doubts— she had done her best, and she would hang on to the peace she had felt just moments before. Her father's oft-repeated words echoed in her mind: *Who knows but that you have come to the kingdom for such a time as this?*

She opened the door, and there stood Hegai, smiling at her. "Yes, my dear, you have chosen well, just as I expected you would." He looked approvingly at her, nodding at the single medallion hanging around her neck against the blue gown. As he led her outside, he said, "As for Misgath, you and Hathach have just rendered a great service to the Crown. She has confessed the plot to poison any candidate who might have had a chance to be queen, and she has been taken to the garrison. She insists she does not know who gave her the poison, but I have my suspicions."

"And Jess—I mean Hathach," Hadassah asked quickly. "How is the young guard doing who saved me from disaster?"

Hegai smiled knowingly and said, "He will fully recover, though he will be in some discomfort for a few days." He led her into the courtyard, where she saw a beautiful golden litter with four strong guards at each corner. He helped her into the conveyance.

"Good-bye, Star, my First Candidate," Hegai said proudly as she seated herself on the velvet cushions and the four men lifted the royal litter to their shoulders.

The palace grounds were enormous, and Hadassah felt like it was taking days to arrive at the king's chambers. She passed by beautifully decorated rooms and more large courtyards filled with people who turned to watch as she passed. She heard excited whispers, "The First Candidate," and ". . . maybe the new queen," and comments about her beauty as the litter moved forward.

Then she saw a beloved face in the crowd. It was Mordecai. She risked a brief wave, and he waved back, his expression full of love and pride and wistfulness for what might have been. Oh, how much she loved him! She craned her neck to see him as long as she could.

Hadassah turned her attention to the journey ahead and the meeting at the end of it.

What is he really like? went through her mind over and over. As much as she had learned from Hegai about the king, she knew there would be characteristics of his personality that only she would discover . . . if she became his wife. *Will he love me and want me for his queen?* she whispered to herself as the high, intricately carved wooden doors in the distance grew larger and the litter began to slow its forward progress.

The guards finally lowered the litter to the ground, and one of them reached for her hand to help Hadassah to a standing position. She lifted her eyes to the top of the door and felt very small and insignificant.

But then she prayed once more, "May your will be done, Lord," and calm filled her and gave her courage. She took one step forward, and two soldiers on each side of the double door grabbed the brass handles and swung them wide.

Hadassah took a deep breath. Thoughts floated through her mind. *You are at the end of all the waiting, the preparation. You are ready to go into the presence of the king!* And she was filled with joy and anticipation. She started forward very slowly, one step in front of the other, into the dimness of the room. She paused a moment to let her eyes adjust to the darkness, and then . . .

CHAPTER TWELVE

THERE WAS THE KING!

He was tall and strong looking, and even more hand-some than Hadassah had realized from seeing him at the banquet and, since then, from the brief glimpses at a distance around the palace grounds. But now he stood watching her with a smile that grew more warm and welcoming with every step as she approached him.

"You are Star," he said as he also moved toward her.

"How . . . how do you know my name?" she asked.

"Oh, I have ways of finding things out," he joked. "I am the king, you know." They both laughed then, until Hadassah looked shyly away.

"Actually," he went on, "your Hegai has been telling me about you, and he said you were next on the list for me to interview."

Hadassah stared up into King Xerxes' face, seeing beyond his attractive looks into the depths of his dark eyes that reflected strength, fearlessness, and intelligence. But she also noticed a deep weariness within them.

"Yes, Star, you are beautiful like a star," he said. His

eyes glanced at the medallion around her neck. "Is that your only jewel, your only adornment? Every other candidate for queen has come weighted down with more gold and jewels than she could manage—as if they were *planning* on being rejected and must by all means collect as many riches as they could carry away from the palace." His expression was both amused and curious.

"Your Majesty, I have learned that when someone has an audience with the king, rather than expecting a gift, you should bring a gift to him. And this"—Hadassah reached up to lift the medallion over her head—"is my gift to you." She held out the necklace in her hands.

"But why, I must ask," Xerxes said, frowning in bewilderment. "I have a treasury full of gold and jewels."

"Because," Hadassah began slowly, "this is all I have. When I give it to you, it means I am bringing you everything. My mind. My heart. All of me."

He did not respond for a long moment, and Hadassah wondered if she had offended him. She took a deep breath to still her quaking body. Then he reached for the medallion and held it up to the light.

"You see, Your Majesty," Hadassah continued, her voice quavering just slightly, "this is a near replica of a medallion given to me on my seventh birthday as gift from my parents. They were killed that same night."

"I'm so sorry to hear of your terrible loss, Star," the king said, and his voice sounded like he truly did care. "Thank

you for this meaningful gift. I have never received such
a . . . such a cherished memento before."

"It is only a symbol, Your Majesty. The gift I most wish
to give to you is myself." Hadassah's heart nearly stopped
beating as she searched his face for some sign of good will
toward her. What if he thought she was too forward,
too. . . ?

"Well, Star, I am most amazed by this interview, this
encounter with a most unusual young woman," his voice
broke into her worried thoughts. "I must admit I am not at
my best this evening. The rigors of the court and the loom-
ing threat of war with Greece—but I'm sure you don't want
to hear about all that." Xerxes shook his head.

"Oh, but I do," Hadassah exclaimed. "I have been
learning about Persia, about you—" She stumbled to a
pause, searching his face for his reaction. When she could
find no indication that he was upset, she went on, "I have
asked Hegai, the chamberlain, to tell me about your personality, what you like and dislike, about your family heritage—everything that has gone into making you who you
are."

"You want to know *me*," he demanded, "or is it the
powerful and rich king you seek to know?"

Hadassah trembled again as she answered, her voice
low, "I want to know the one who is the king and the one
who is the man. All of you."

King Xerxes bent his head to hear the last whispered

words. He shook his head, a look of amazement on his face. "I do not know why I am admitting this to you, Star, but I am not sure I know the difference between the man and the king." His voice also dropped as he finished his confession.

"Perhaps I can help you find yourself again," Star offered quietly.

Something deep within the man seemed to have been touched by the simple words, and Xerxes, the ruler of the known world, reached out a hand to touch Hadassah's cheek. "Yes, perhaps you can, dear Star."

Hadassah's hand slowly moved up to touch his against her cheek, and he turned her hand over and kissed the palm.

A knock on the door brought both of them around to face it, and the king's Master of Audiences, Memucan, appeared, looking apologetic. "I am sorry, Your Majesty, but there is an urgent matter."

"Ah yes, Memucan," said the king, sounding both exasperated and resigned. "I will be there in a moment." He turned to Hadassah and said, "Thank you again, Star, for your gift and for what it symbolizes." His hand touched her cheek once more, and he was gone.

Hadassah felt a mixture of joy and bewilderment as

Hegai quietly led her away, this time out a private back way with no golden litter. The king had seemed genuinely grateful and tender, but their time together was over so abruptly. . . .

The chamberlain, who had become a friend, almost a second father to her, looked into her face but asked no questions. He stopped in front of an unfamiliar door and explained, "You may stay here in private for a while, until the king. . . ." But his voice trailed off, mirroring the uncertainty Hadassah was feeling. "Don't worry, my little Star," he added as he looked into her eyes. "I am confident all is well and the king will choose wisely. Just give him some time."

Hadassah smiled weakly and entered the small private room. She looked around and quickly realized all her personal belongings had been transferred to it while she had been with the king. She sank onto the bed, her face buried in her hands. "Oh, God, please help me to trust you in all this uncertainty. Help me to wait patiently. . . ." A sob caught in her throat.

Her petition to the Lord was one she had to repeat daily. Days passed with no word from the king, no hint of his intentions. Hadassah slept fitfully, and food had little appeal. Hegai urged her to eat to keep up her strength, to be ready. . . .

Ready for what? Hadassah snapped angrily to herself at those times when God seemed very far away and her uncertain future loomed darkly in her imagination. *He probably has chosen someone else by now,* she told herself in her worst moments, her heart feeling like a stone in her chest.

But then Hegai came to tell her that the king had been required to leave in order to address an urgent problem in a distant province, and he would not have had time even to think about deciding on a queen. Hadassah's heart lifted a bit. *So there is a reason he has not called for me,* she thought. *I wonder if he even remembers our so brief time together,* she asked herself many times each day.

When she was most discouraged, a favorite Scripture would urge her to faith and confidence in her heavenly King. But by the time one moon's cycle had passed, Hadassah needed every ounce of willpower and every Scripture passage she had ever memorized to keep herself from sinking into despair.

For a while Hadassah tried to prepare herself each morning for the possibility of that royal summons, choosing her gown, combing her hair, and artfully using the cosmetics with which she had experimented for so many months. But after a while it seemed simply a useless waste of time, and she would throw on a wrinkled homespun wrap and drag herself outside to the pool area. At times she was able to talk herself into reading one of the scrolls Hegai had brought her, and she was glad to discover her mind had focused on something other than the king's silence for a period of time.

She was lying on a lounge by the pool one morning when she glanced over her shoulder to find the reason for a commotion by the courtyard gate. She could see a length of purple tapestry held aloft by slender poles over the head of someone important, obviously a court official of high rank surrounded by guards. She quickly sat up. *Has the king returned? Has he decided. . . ?* But she could not even finish the thought.

Several of the candidates gathered to see what was happening, and one of them, a tall, lovely girl from Phrygia, moved discreetly into the path of the official. He marched directly toward this woman, Carylina. Hadassah's heart sank as she rose to her feet. *The king has decided, and he has not chosen me,* mournfully wound its way through her being. Her knees felt like they had turned to water, and she nearly collapsed onto her lounge. She felt almost more sad for Mordecai and for Jesse than for herself. *All those discussions about divine destiny, about coming to the kingdom for a special reason . . .*

Then Hadassah nearly stopped breathing as she watched the king's Master of Audiences, Memucan, place his hand on Carylina's shoulder and slowly move her aside in order to walk straight toward . . . Hadassah!

She quickly glanced over her shoulder to see if someone else was intended for whatever Memucan's message was, but no one was behind her. The man moved to within a few steps of Hadassah, then knelt before her with a bow. She felt as though she had turned to marble. Before she could think of what to say, he looked up at her. "My lady with the name Star, your presence is desired at the court of His Majesty King Xerxes of Persia. Would you honor me with your hand?"

The world seemed to fall into a total stillness. Even Hadassah's racing heart had slowed, like a leaf gliding to the surface of a pond as the wind died away. *He remembered my name,* was the thought that filled her heart with unbelievable joy.

As Hadassah slowly reached out her hand to take Memucan's, a sound like water filled the air, and she realized it was applause. As she looked around, she discovered the candidates who had filled the courtyard to watch the proceedings were clapping for her. Again her knees nearly gave out on her, and Memucan held her upright and led her toward the courtyard gate.

"What . . . do you know. . . ?" Hadassah tried to ask him a question, but he shook his head silently though with a reassuring smile. As they approached the gate, she saw a golden litter, even larger and more ornate than the one she had ridden in before. *Was it only a month ago?* she asked herself in awe. It seemed like years.

And then she saw that one of the litter-bearers was . . . Jesse! She could hardly contain her joy at seeing him, and she nearly gave away their friendship as she started to call out his name. But he gave a quick warning shake of his head, and Hadassah took a deep breath to help control her emotions. She prayed, *Thank you, Lord, for allowing Jesse to make this journey with me. Thank you for his care for me through all that has happened to him. Bless him today....*

Memucan helped her into the beautiful conveyance. *But I am not ready!* she said to herself in panic as she looked down at her clothing. Her ordinary coarse tunic was a stark contrast to the splendor of the litter and was hardly appropriate for an audience with the king.

But as soon as she was seated, a tapestry was drawn around all sides of the carrier, and she realized a lovely set of royal robes were folded in place and ready for her to put on. Then a maid ducked inside the litter with an array of cosmetics and began to adorn her face and hair. Someone had even thought to include her heirloom medallion, and she silently thanked Hegai in her heart as she gratefully slipped it over her head.

The maid smiled and clapped her approval as she leaned back to inspect Hadassah, then slipped quickly away. Unseen hands pulled the curtain back, and Hadassah looked out over a sea of faces turned her way. A new round of applause filled the air, and the four guards, including Jesse, lifted the litter and started forward, Memucan in the lead.

The canopy over the litter shaded Hadassah from the

sun, and servants ran alongside waving palm branches for a refreshing breeze. The crowds moved toward the procession, and she was shocked to see them bowing to her as she passed.

The journey across the palace grounds seemed to take even longer than it had before. Hadassah took deep breaths to calm herself, then began to pray, first the familiar words of the Shema, then her own heartfelt petition for the Lord to be with her, to give her wisdom and caution when she needed it, boldness and courage at other times.

She opened her eyes to see directly ahead of her—Papa Mordecai! Her eyes filled with tears of joy as she waved and mouthed a greeting to him. His face was full of emotion, some of it bittersweet she knew, as they both now realized the absolute certainty of never being able to go back to the way their life had been.

Mordecai was soon out of sight, and Hadassah saw they were now entering a magnificent hall. High pillars reflected sunlight streaming down onto a carpet of scarlet stretching into the distance. A battalion of the king's personal bodyguards lined each side up to that same high wooden doorway she had entered when she had first met him in person. Her heart was pounding so hard she wondered if others would hear it.

At a command from Memucan, the litter was lowered to the floor in front of the door. This time it was already wide open. She heard a whispered, "Go with God," from

Jesse as Memucan held Hadassah's arm to help her alight from the litter. "His Majesty awaits you, Your Highness," he said.

What did he call me? raced through Hadassah's mind. *"Your Highness?"* She still could hardly believe it was happening. She moved slowly toward the doorway, trying to see into the shadows of the room beyond.

CHAPTER THIRTEEN

AND ONCE MORE KING XERXES STOOD BEFORE HAD-
assah, his welcoming smile going straight to her heart. She
began to move more quickly, and suddenly the long month
of uncertainty, of waiting, of wondering what would happen
all gathered together into this one moment, and Hadassah
could wait no longer. She ran the last few steps into the
king's arms. He lifted her up and swung her around, and
they both were laughing with joy.

"My Star, my queen!" Xerxes nearly shouted as the
doors were swiftly and quietly closed behind them. He held
her in his arms and looked at the medallion around her
neck. "Look," he said, "I am wearing mine, too."

Hadassah reached out to touch the six-pointed star as it
lay against Xerxes' chest. "Is that how you remembered my
name?" she asked softly.

He laughed again as he set her down on her feet. "Star,
I would never forget your name. I have thought of you
nearly every moment during this long month away. Actually, I was also thinking about how I would convince my
advisors that I did not have to wed someone from a noble

family, which is the tradition around here. But I have decided I don't need to convince them." He grinned in rather wicked amusement. "I'm more than convinced, and that's good enough for me."

He turned serious and looked intently into her face. "I do want you for my queen and wife, Star."

Hadassah moved into the circle of his arms and whispered, "Yes," against his neck.

"I will call you Esther, 'E-star,' the beautiful star and Queen of Persia," Xerxes continued, "mistress of all the land between the Nile and the Indus. Let all who live under my rule hold you dear in their hearts. You are from henceforth Persia's queen and my wife."

"'Esther,'" Hadassah repeated softly. "Yes, I accept my new name and my new position as your wife."

Their arms intertwined once more, and the kiss that sealed their private marriage ceremony was full of love and hope for the future.

Later that day, Xerxes led Esther up a long flight of stairs to a balcony overlooking a huge courtyard filled with citizens of the Persian kingdom. When the balcony doors were opened and the king and his new queen appeared before the crowd, a deafening roar filled the air as people shouted their delight and exclaimed over the new queen's beauty.

The king raised her hand in his, and the noise quieted. "I present to you my queen, and she will be called by her Persian name, Queen Esther!" And the crowd again shouted and clapped their excitement and approval.

"Queen Esther! Queen Esther!" turned into a chant as the Persians welcomed their new queen and bowed before the two standing high above them. A stooped, white-bearded old man stepped forward from the doorway behind them carrying something weighty in his hands. At a signal from Xerxes, the new queen knelt and a gold crown encrusted with jewels was settled on her shining dark hair. The crowd's roar was deafening.

Esther stood and looked quickly over the faces below them, then back again. *If only Papa . . .* and then she saw him, waving and laughing and shouting along with the rest. She could hardly wait till they could talk, and this time they wouldn't have to speak through the bars on the gate. She was the Queen of Persia, and she would be able to see Mordecai nearly any time she wanted to!

Queen Esther did not have to wait long—the next day she asked her maid to arrange for her father to be brought to her, and soon they stood face to face, hands clasped together, trying to find words for the emotions they were feeling.

"Oh, daughter," Mordecai was finally able to say, his voice choked, "I am so proud of you, so glad you prepared yourself for this moment. The God of Abraham, Isaac, and

Jacob has been with you all this time, protecting you when you also could have been killed along with your parents, guiding me as I raised you to love Him, and shielding and inspiring you as you disciplined your body, mind, and spirit to be ready for the king's choice."

"Yes, Papa," Esther answered, her own voice full of tears. "God has indeed been with me. Through your prayers for me and through your wise counsel as we met each day at the gate, I am here." She wrapped her arms around his neck and kissed his cheek.

"I can hardly believe what has happened," she added, and they both laughed in spite of the emotion of the moment.

Then Mordecai turned serious, and he said, "Hadassah—I mean Queen Esther." They chuckled again. "Whatever God has planned for you has only begun. You must continue to watch, listen, and be ready for anything He wants you to do or say."

Esther nodded solemnly and said, "Yes, my father, I do want to stay alert and ready. And I will be calling on you as before for your wisdom and experience."

"And remember our secret, Hadassah. You have not told the king, have you?" asked Mordecai.

"No, Papa," she assured him. "I have kept my ancestry hidden, although if you keep calling me 'Hadassah' it may not matter," she finished with a little smile.

Mordecai's answering smile was rueful, and he said,

"Yes, you are Queen Esther now, though you will always be my Hadassah in my heart."

She hugged him again as he turned to go. "I'll see you soon," she promised. She walked with him to the door of her quarters, and as she waved good-bye, something on the back of one of her own guards filled her with sudden dread. There it was—*the twisted cross!* Being the queen was not the entirely safe place she had assumed it would be.

Esther soon discovered there were lots of things about being queen that weren't very interesting or rewarding. Though she could have nearly anything she desired simply by making her request known, she had never been one for exotic foods, and she already had all the royal gowns and jewels she could ever want. King Xerxes had to be away a lot, dealing with the issues of his far-flung empire and planning strategies to fend off the enemies of Persia. The times the king and queen did have together were all the more precious, but she wished he were at home in the palace more often. Her father continued with his job as scribe, so even he was not as available as she would have liked. And he cautioned her that they should not meet too often in case somebody would start nosing around and discover her Jewish heritage.

She was often lonely, even though there were many

people around the palace. But they all seemed to be busy with their own duties, and she sometimes wondered to herself, *If God has put me in this position, why doesn't He show me what I'm supposed to be doing?*

When she complained about it to Mordecai at one of their private meetings, he listened carefully, then took her hand and said, "We never know exactly what our Father has in mind for each day, and sometimes He simply wants us to say a kind word to someone or give to someone in need. But each of those times we obey His quiet voice in our hearts, we are preparing ourselves for the really big thing He might have in mind for us to do."

"Papa, I don't know what I would do without you," Esther said with a smile and a hug. "You are so wise and—"

"Shhh," Mordecai said, putting a finger on her lips. "Only God is truly wise. I, too, am still learning also how to listen and obey."

After praying together, he left Esther to return to his work at the gates of the palace.

When Mordecai finished his last parchment for the day, he leaned his head back against the wall, and closed his eyes to pray once more for his beloved daughter. He, too, wondered what God had in mind for her, but his counsel to her about trusting God and obeying Him echoed in his mind and was a comfort to his own soul.

His attention eventually was caught by two guards on the wall above him—they must have thought he was asleep, because from what he was hearing they were discussing a plan to kill the king!

One of them said, his voice gruff, "It has to be tonight, just after he has dinner with the queen. He leaves tomorrow for battle, and he's decided to take our leader with him! Our man must be here to take over the throne. So is your blade sharp? Are you ready to die for the cause?"

Mordecai couldn't hear a response, but he was sure it was positive because the guards chuckled in an evil way and moved on.

Mordecai held as still as he could, keeping his eyes shut tight, and when he was sure the guards were gone, he slowly got to his feet, yawning and stretching as if nothing was wrong. As quickly as he could without drawing attention to himself, he approached the queen's chambers and asked for an audience with Esther.

When she appeared, Mordecai quickly whispered to her what he had overheard. Esther went faint with shock, and Mordecai urged her to immediately warn the king.

Thinking quickly, Esther sent someone to bring Memucan to her. He would be able to swiftly mobilize another battalion of loyal soldiers to surround the king and keep him safe from the attack. And her relationship with Mordecai would remain hidden.

"But I will find a way to let the king know it is you who saved his life," Esther said to Mordecai before they parted. "This will help you gain his trust."

"No, no, leave me out of it," Mordecai argued. But Esther insisted, assuring him that she would be very discreet in how the information was relayed to the king.

As soon as Memucan arrived at her quarters, she urgently told him of the conspiracy to kill Xerxes, and the official didn't wait around to hear an explanation of her source before hurrying away to protect the king.

Later that evening, as the king and queen ate their meal together, Xerxes asked her about the threat he'd heard about from Memucan. "He told me the warning had come through you," he said, looking very curious.

Esther paused a moment to gather her thoughts, then answered, "Yes, I will tell you in confidence. An . . . an old family friend named Mordecai informed me. He is a court scribe and overheard the wicked plot." Esther couldn't keep the tremble out of her voice as she finished. She clasped Xerxes' hand between both of hers, knowing he would be leaving in the morning to fight the Greeks and wondering when she would see him again. *After all this, will my beloved husband be killed anyway?* flashed unbidden through her mind, but she would not allow herself to dwell further on the terrible thought.

"This story will be included in the Chronicles of the Kings," Xerxes was saying as she turned her attention back to him, "and I must think of how this man—Mordecai, you say his name is?—can be rewarded."

But the king indeed left the next day, and nothing was done about recognizing Mordecai's heroic deed.

CHAPTER FOURTEEN

MORDECAI HAD AN ENEMY ALSO. HIS NAME TURNED out to be Haman the Agagite, and he had grown in power next to the king himself. While Xerxes was out fighting the Greeks, this man had gone with him, distinguishing himself during the various battles with his astute advice and strategic command of each combat situation.

Xerxes discovered that Haman was also very wealthy. What the King did *not* know is that Haman's marauding bands had continued to plunder and kill all over the empire while Haman kept himself close to the king, currying favor at court as well as in battle. Neither did the king know that Haman's wealth nearly surpassed that of the royal treasury.

Esther heard from Memucan that the Persian army was on its way home, and her heart leaped in her chest at the thought she soon would see her beloved Xerxes! She and Mordecai stood out on the palace balcony, watching the horizon as the dust of thousands of men and horses drew near. Finally she was able to make out the form of her husband, the king, riding at the head of his exhausted, battle-worn men. He raised his head and looked into her face, a smile softening the weary lines on his own face.

As he rode out of sight through the palace gates, Esther quickly turned to rush down the steps to him. But out of the corner of her eye she saw once more . . . *the twisted cross emblem!* She clutched Mordecai's arm in terror, and she knew by his expression he had seen it.

"Papa," she whispered, "have you seen that symbol before? Do you know what it means?"

But he already was nodding grimly. "Yes, my daughter, I'm afraid I do," he said.

A whole battalion of men riding on horseback and led by a large man—a familiar face around the court, but Esther was not able to immediately recall his name—were coolly wearing the same symbol.

She and Mordecai simply looked wordlessly at each other, then turned to the stairs.

Esther found Xerxes in his chambers, shedding his dusty armor. His smile was warm but tired, and he suggested she might want to wait to embrace him until after his bath. But Esther could not wait and threw her arms around him.

"Oh, my beloved, I have been so worried—"

He put a finger up to her lips, then kissed her, and no more words were needed.

While they were having their meal together that

evening, the first in many months, Memucan asked for a brief audience with the king, apologizing for the intrusion, "but the matter is urgent," he explained. Esther offered to excuse herself, but Xerxes put up his hand to signal she should stay.

"Well, my lord, I am afraid I have some rather grave news," Memucan began. "With the expenses of the war and all—" he paused a moment—"well, the king's treasury has been depleted."

Xerxes shouted, "What do you mean, 'depleted'? What has happened to it? How could you, my most trusted advisor, have allowed it to . . ." But his voice drifted to a stop, and he buried his face in his hands as he realized the foolishness of blaming Memucan.

Memucan quickly began describing some cost-saving measures he had already thought of, along with a further tax from each of the provinces, ". . . and very soon the coffers will again be full. I've already been collecting gold and jewelry wherever I can—calling in debts from the provinces. They of course are complaining, but I'll find some way to settle everyone down again," he assured the king.

Esther leaned forward and began rather timidly, "I have an idea, too." The two men turned to her in some astonishment as she described a women-only event in which she would hold court and hear their problems, large and small, and advise the women on courses of action. This would keep them and their husbands loyal to the king, she said,

"And there may be advice from some of the women there that might help," she added quickly as she finished.

"Splendid, my queen!" exclaimed Xerxes with enthusiasm. "You will help Memucan hold the kingdom together while I am away. And I do hope it will not be so long this time. I missed you," he said softly as Memucan quietly took his leave of the king and queen.

Early the next morning a soft knocking was heard on the royal bedchamber door. Xerxes turned over with a groan and muttered something to Esther about just ignoring it, but the knock came again.

"What is it?" shouted the king. "This better be good."

The door cracked open, and Esther nearly gasped with astonishment when she saw who it was. *Jesse!*

"Excuse me, Your Majesty," his voice quavered, "but it is my sad duty to inform you that Memucan, the Master of Audiences, has . . . has been murdered," he finished in a rush.

"*No-o-o-o!*" Esther heard the wail from her husband as he leaped from the bed, then fell to his knees on the floor. She rushed to his side to comfort him, but he seemed beyond coherent thought. Finally he lifted his head and demanded, "Have the murderers been caught yet?"

Jesse, known as Hathach, shook his head wordlessly,

then said, "All we know is that Memucan was stabbed to death as he slept last night. We have found no evidence except this cloak that must have been dropped as the perpetrators fled." Jesse held it up, and the morning light caught the emblem embroidered on the back—once again, the cross with the broken arms had come to haunt Esther's dreams and turn them into nightmares.

Xerxes had taken his sorrowful leave of Esther later that morning for the scheduled trip he could not postpone, leaving Hathach, her friend Jesse, in charge of investigating Memucan's murder.

It was much later when Esther discovered that one of the king's princes, that man named Haman, had sent a letter to the king with this announcement: He, Haman, was very grateful for the opportunity to serve Persia and its king, both in battle and as part of the royal court. He was very sorry at the king's loss of Memucan, he wrote, but now it was time for him to "give back" to the empire, to offer his experience and his wealth as the new Master of Audiences. . . .

When Xerxes returned to his court, he made a public introduction of his new Master of Audiences, Haman the Agagite. "It is my will that each of you obey and treat him in every way exactly as you would regard your king," he told the crowd.

Esther was nearly struck dumb with terror as she realized what was happening. Her husband was being taken in by a man who was an enemy of her people, the Jews. And how could she explain all this to Xerxes without giving away the secret she had promised Mordecai she would guard with her life? She spent many sleepless nights thinking about it all and praying for help from God. *What should I do?* filled her mind nearly every waking minute.

The king had even given Haman his own ring as a symbol of the man's position in the kingdom. Haman was a man transformed by the accolades and attention, and he wanted all of Persia to honor him and bow before him. When he passed through the gates of the palace, his guards shouted, "Everyone bow before His Excellency, the king's Master of Audiences, Haman the Agagite! All must stand and bow!" they called their instructions over and over.

At once the hundreds of onlookers stood and bowed at the waist, just as they would do before the king himself. Except for Mordecai. He simply sat as still as a statue at his scribe's desk by the gate.

One of the guards moved over to Mordecai, brandishing his sword. "Haven't you heard, you idiot?" he shouted into Mordecai's face. "There is a new Master of Audiences, and the king has decreed you must honor him as you would the king himself!" Mordecai didn't move a muscle, refusing to even look at the nearly hysterical man. The guard finally swore at him and strode off.

Haman's chariot was close behind, and his eyes fastened on Mordecai, now back at work with pen and scroll. Haman swiveled his head to stare at him until his chariot had turned the corner.

A fellow scribe whispered loudly, "What's the matter with you, Mordecai? Why did you disobey the king's direct order?"

"I bow to no man but to my God, the Most High, and to my king, Xerxes," he said, his answer low but his tone unyielding.

"Who is this God, this one for whom your loyalty could get you into enormous trouble?" asked his friend.

Mordecai paused, thinking about Esther and the secret he had made her guard all this time, then made the decision he had known would come sooner or later. "I worship Jehovah, the Creator of heaven and earth. The God of Abraham, Isaac, and Jacob," he said in a loud, clear voice.

Mordecai had announced that he was a Jew.

Haman had ridden away from the palace gate extremely angry, and when the same situation with Mordecai happened several days in a row, Haman was fit to be tied. He stalked around trying to figure out how he could make that stiff-necked scribe pay in blood for his stubbornness.

Then one of Haman's men brought him some news. He'd heard through the grapevine that *Mordecai was a Jew*, that he worshiped the Lord God of Abraham, Isaac, and Jacob. Haman became even more livid with rage.

"Who does he think he is?" he shouted to those who were cowering in his presence. But then his anger took an even darker turn, and he grinned wickedly. He would come up with a scheme. Finally he had the grounds on which to launch his wholesale slaughter of the Jews. He would have his revenge on that long-ago King Saul and the battle that had wiped out most of Haman's forebears. And he would get rid of this pious Jew-pig at the same time!

Haman came into the presence of King Xerxes the next morning, putting on an expression of deep distress. The king wanted to know what the matter was with his new Master of Audiences. Haman pretended to be extremely reluctant to be the bearer of bad tidings, but eventually he told the king, "Your Majesty, I have uncovered a massive conspiracy against you. I have discovered that it began with the killing of Memucan, and I have evidence that a large ethnic group called Jews who live in a section of the city not too far from the palace are planning to kill you and overthrow the Persian kingdom."

Of course by now he had King Xerxes' full attention, and Haman went on, "Today I passed one of them, a scribe in your own court, who tells anyone who will listen that he gives obeisance to only his own god. He openly flaunts his refusal to bow to me, and it could just as well be you."

"Who is this Jew?" shouted Xerxes. "Is he in custody?"

"No, Your Majesty. I did not want to tip off any of his co-conspirators that we are on to them."

"I have known and worked with Jews all my life," said the king, shaking his head. "What a betrayal. My own grandfather allowed many of them to return to Israel with Ezra to rebuild their temple."

"Exactly!" exclaimed Haman. "This is how they repay the king's generosity—with plots and treachery."

So by unjustly blaming the Jews for things they had not done, Haman tricked the king into signing a terrible decree. Haman laughed with evil glee as he had his men cast the *pur*, lots to determine the exact day for his massacre of the Jews to be carried out. The winning lot was the thirteenth day of Adar, when all the Jews in Persia were to be killed by any Persian citizens who were inclined to do so, and their homes and businesses could be plundered, as well.

Haman summoned all the palace scribes into his presence. Each scribe was assigned to write the king's decrees in a specific language used in the various countries comprising the Persian Empire, and as Mordecai heard the first words of the decree, his heart felt as if it had turned to stone.

"On the thirteenth day of the month of Adar, all citizens of Persia are to destroy, to kill, every person of Jewish blood. . . ." Mordecai's hand trembled as he tried to write the terrible words.

"Does . . . does this edict actually come from the king?" asked a brave scribe in the front row. "Does it bear the king's seal, his royal signet?"

Haman stared at the questioner, then held up his hand with a grim smile, allowing the king's ring to glitter in the light. Then he slammed the jewel and its seal down on the scribe's parchment, indenting the document with the royal seal.

"*Now* it does," he announced triumphantly, staring across the heads in front of him to Mordecai in the back row.

By the king's own royal horsemen, the decree was sent out to all 127 provinces of Persia, from India in the east to Ethiopia in the west.

CHAPTER FIFTEEN

QUEEN ESTHER, UNAWARE THAT ALL THIS WAS GOING on, was reading in her room when her maid came to her with a message. There was someone to see her out in the corridor. When Esther went to see who it was, there was her friend Jesse!

"I can't believe it!" she exclaimed. "I haven't seen you for ages—"

"I have news, Hadassah—I mean Queen Esther," Jesse interrupted. He explained he didn't have much time and had come with an important message from Mordecai. He looked so serious that Esther immediately felt concerned.

"What is it, Jesse?" she asked, worry in her voice.

"Mordecai asked me to tell you something." Then Jesse stepped closer so only she could hear and told her about the king's new edict. Esther, shocked, stepped back with her face in her hands. Jesse waited until she had regained some control of her emotions, then went on to explain that Mordecai had dressed in sackcloth and poured ashes on his head to show how sorrowful and grief-stricken he was because of what was going to happen to the Jews.

"He wants you to go to the king and plead for the life of your people," Jesse said slowly, looking into Esther's face.

"Oh, Jesse," she cried, "you know I can't do that! You know the law—only a person who has been called into the presence of the king may appear there. If the king doesn't summon that one—even me—and hold out his scepter, he or she will be killed! I'm so frightened—"

But Jesse interrupted, "Hadassah—for you always will be Hadassah to me—Mordecai told me to tell you this, and he made me repeat the words to him to make sure I had it right. He said, 'Do not think, Hadassah, that because you are in the king's house, you alone of all the Jews will escape. If you remain silent now, God will surely raise a deliverer for His people. But you and your father's house will perish forever.'" Jesse paused a moment and looked Esther straight in the eyes. "Mordecai said to say to you, 'Who knows, Hadassah, but maybe you have come to the palace for such a time as this?'"

With fear choking her voice, Esther said, "Tell my

father I will do as he says. Ask him to gather the Jews of the city together to fast and pray for three days, and I and my maidens will do the same. I will go to the king. And if I perish, I perish."

Esther was shaking with fear as she found her way back to her quarters. She took a deep breath, silently asked God for help, and gathered her maids around her to instruct them on the preparation for her audience with the king. They were all fearful, too, and they begged her not to go. But they soon saw that none of their words would persuade her away from her determination to go before the king, even if it resulted in her death.

After the three days of fasting and prayer were completed, Esther's maidens helped her bathe and dress in her queenly robes. Tears silently ran down their faces as they said good-bye and wished her well. They were certain they would never see her again.

"It has been decades since someone has gone into the king without being called," one of them argued once more. But their queen simply lifted her hand for silence.

Esther looked around at the weeping group. "I have no certainty of the outcome," she said slowly, "but I am sure I am doing the right thing. I also am certain that Jehovah God will be with me."

Esther couldn't help but remember that original long

journey for her first audience with the king. Would this time have as joyful an outcome? She shivered as she approached the entrance to the inner court of the palace, then took a deep breath to calm herself. "I am yours, Lord, and I am here to do your bidding. Again, may your will be done."

She stopped before the open door into the inner court and waited for her eyes to adjust from the strong sunshine outside to the cool dimness in front of her. She took a deep breath along with her first step over the threshold. The vast room was full of supplicants and bureaucrats hoping for the king's ear.

King Xerxes was sitting on his throne, facing the entrance to the royal court. Gradually those near the doorway recognized Queen Esther, and a few gasps followed, as they obviously remembered palace protocol along with the fate of the previous queen, Vashti.

Eventually the whole place went silent as people watched Queen Esther slowly moving along the red carpet.

Then, almost as one, they turned to look at the king, holding their breath. Would he hold out his scepter, or would she be dragged away to her death?

Esther whispered one last prayer, "O Father, I want no other outcome than the one that furthers your plans for your people, the Jews. Please do not let me take a single step or say a single word outside your will."

Now only a few steps away from the king's dais, Esther lifted her eyes to his, searching for any hint of what he was thinking and feeling. His expression was questioning, but he did not seem angry, she determined with some relief.

And then a most unexpected reaction came from deep within Esther's heart. *This is my husband, the one I love,* she thought, and her lips curved into a smile.

"And why do you smile at me, my queen?" he leaned forward to ask in a low voice. "Most people at such a moment of intrusion would be ready to faint with fear." Esther's eyes moved to his fist gripping the scepter. That arm had not moved a muscle.

"Because, Your Majesty," she answered him, her voice also soft, "even at this moment of highest danger, of which I am well aware, your presence fills me with joy. I am overwhelmed when I come close to the one I love."

There was a long moment when time seemed to have stopped. The enormous courtroom was absolutely silent as the audience watched the drama unfold.

Then the king stood and smiled at Esther and held out

the golden scepter. Everyone, including Esther, slowly let out their breaths as she began to walk up the steps to the king. When she was in front of the throne, she reached out her hand to touch the king's scepter, still extended toward her.

"What is it, Queen Esther? What is it that you want?" he asked, his voice now raised so those in the farthest corners could hear. "Even if you request half the kingdom of Persia, it will be granted to you." The audience immediately began a shocked clamor at such a promise, and they looked at the queen with awe. What power she had with the king!

"If it would please the king," Esther said, her voice clear, "I request that you come to a banquet I have prepared. And if you please, bring Haman as our guest." The crowd again buzzed with this unusual request. But the king, though at a loss as to the reason, nodded his agreement and sent word to Haman of his good fortune.

Before the king could ask any further questions, Esther excused herself to prepare for the evening's event and walked back up the red carpet, holding her swirl of emotions in check and looking as queenly as she could.

CHAPTER SIXTEEN

ESTHER QUICKLY ASSEMBLED HER PRIVATE COOKS
and her maids to help prepare a wonderful meal of pheasant, kebabs of beef and hen, roasted vegetables, and exotic desserts prepared from cooking methods and ingredients gathered across the kingdom.

Esther selected a high balcony overlooking the grounds of the palace with a view of the setting sun. Under her direction, her maids arranged the three lounges around the table and decorated the area with baskets of flowers. Fans of palm fronds were placed at the ready in case the evening breezes did not sufficiently cool the area.

Esther checked once more to make sure the table settings and every food item were just so. And then she heard the king and their guest on the stairs. She moved toward them with a smile, keeping her eyes fastened on her husband's. She made herself be a gracious hostess to Haman, though her heart quaked again with fear and anger when she thought of his evil plan.

But she kept her voice even and courteous as she

invited Haman to recline at the table and enjoy the banquet.

"This is most delicious," Haman told her as he filled his plate for the third time.

"Yes, indeed, my dear," Xerxes agreed. "Maybe I'll trade cooks with you," he laughed.

Esther smiled her response, watching the two men and measuring the moment. But Haman was refilling his goblet with wine and wolfing it down so quickly she became alarmed. The man had started out the evening very jovial and talkative, no doubt thrilled with this intimate evening in the presence of the most powerful ruler in the known world and his beautiful queen. But now Haman's speech was slurred, and he seemed to be nearly asleep on his lounge chair.

The king finished his meal and raised his goblet toward Esther. "Now, my queen, your request. It will indeed be granted unto you, even if it is half the kingdom."

Esther paused for a moment, glanced at the intoxicated man across the table, then said, "Actually, if I have found favor with the king, and if it pleases you to grant my petition, I would humbly ask that you and Haman join me tomorrow night for another banquet." The king looked surprised, but Esther quickly added, "Then I will present to you my request."

Xerxes looked deeply into Esther's eyes, then slowly nodded his agreement. He had to speak rather loudly to get

Haman's attention and announce to him the second invitation.

In spite of his current state, Haman was aware enough to be overjoyed at being singled out for special recognition by the queen herself and invited for a second evening in a row. The king called for a guard to escort the man out to his waiting chariot. And as Haman was driven through the palace gates to return to his home, his bleary eyes fastened on a lone man, dressed in sackcloth, his face and body blackened with ashes, head bowed in prayer. Haman staggered forward in the chariot and shook his fist. "I will destroy you, you Jew pig! Just you wait!"

The conveyance lurched into the street, and Haman lost his footing and collapsed to the floor. All his exhilaration about his evening at a royal banquet was left behind at the palace gate.

By the time he got home, he was in an enormous rage about that "moldy little worm that refuses to recognize my power and influence, given to me directly from the king himself!"

Haman was in such a state that his wife, Zeresh, was getting worried about him. She put her hand on his arm. "Now there, Haman my husband, do not let this creature rob you of your enjoyment of your new position with the king. Maybe now is the time to put all that immense influence to good use."

"What are you suggesting?" Haman asked, turning to stare at Zeresh.

"Well," she said, a hand stroking her chin thoughtfully, "how about having a gallows built tonight, right here near our house, and in the morning you can make a convincing case to the king that—what's his name, Mordecai?—be executed on it."

Within moments Haman was shouting at workmen to prepare the longest, tallest gallows ever seen in the city. No one would ever disrespect him again.

That night the king had a dreadful time sleeping. He'd eaten too much of the delicious food, and he kept wondering what on earth his wife was going to request. He could tell from her rather mysterious manner that it was something important, but he didn't have a clue what it could be.

Tossing and turning, he finally called for a large, mostly boring book that recorded all the events of his reign. The scribe read on and on from the Chronicles of the King while the restless Xerxes tried to doze off. His eyelids had begun to close when suddenly he sat up, fully alert, and asked the man to read the section again.

"'. . . that Mordecai has on this day rendered an exemplary service by thwarting an attempt on the life of the king,'" read the scribe. And so Xerxes was reminded of the time Mordecai brought the warning to Esther about the wicked plot to kill the king and saved the king's life.

"Has Mordecai been honored and rewarded for this brave deed?" the king demanded.

The scribe carefully scanned the parchment. "No, Your Majesty, nothing has been done."

"I left for war with Greece shortly after that," the king remembered aloud. "I have not recognized this man who risked himself. . . ." His voice trailed off, and he stared unseeing into the distance, his mind now churning with this oversight and how to remedy it.

He dismissed the scribe and lay back in his bed, but he did not sleep.

"Who is around here in the court?" the king wanted to know when he arose at dawn from his sleepless night. His servant quickly went to check and returned with the news that Haman had just walked into the area. "Ah, good, just the man I need! Bring the Master of Audiences to me," the king instructed.

Haman was feeling very pleased with himself that morning. He had nearly as much authority in Persia as the king himself! And now the king no doubt was again looking for advice from his second-in-command. Besides, Haman's wife had presented him with a first-rate idea to get rid of that arrogant old Jew. Haman was going to ask the king's permission to execute Mordecai that very day.

Haman couldn't help but smile as he entered the king's chambers and bowed low. "Yes, Your Highness, how may I serve you this morning?" he said.

"I need your advice on something," the king answered. Haman's chest swelled with pride. It was just as he had thought. "What should I do for a man I would especially like to honor?" the king asked.

Haman quickly thought, *Whom would the king rather honor than me?* He crossed his arms over his chest and pretended to ponder the question. Eventually he said to the king, "Let's see, how about one of the royal robes you have worn, and one of your own horses—and let's put the royal crest on the horse's head for all to see. And, hmmm—let's select one of the king's royal princes to lead this fortunate man through the streets of the city, shouting, 'This is what is done for the man the king delights to honor!'"

"Yes," said Xerxes, nodding his head slowly. "Yes, that would certainly be a lavish show of gratitude. That is exactly what I need."

Haman had all he could do to keep from laughing with glee. "It is my honor to serve you, Your Majesty," he said with another low bow.

"Indeed, those are great ideas," the king told Haman. "Go get the robe from my servant, and send someone to the stables for my best horse, and do just as you have suggested."

Haman had started to turn away on his assignment when he heard the king continue, "I want this done for Mordecai, the scribe who sits at the palace gate. I want you to go before him, shouting loudly as my Master of Audiences, 'This is what is done for the man the king delights to honor!' Don't overlook any detail of your fine recommendations." The king did not seem to notice that Haman had suddenly gone pale and speechless.

The bewildered man tried to get his wits about him to ask if there wasn't some terrible mistake. But before he could think of how to ask it, the king motioned Haman on his way. "Be sure to call loudly enough," the king instructed the befuddled man as he stumbled out to do the king's bidding.

Poor Mordecai, weak from hunger and wearing sackcloth, was hardly in any condition for a celebration and a
royal procession through the streets of the Persian capital.
And Haman did not dare mistreat him in light of the
king's instructions. Mordecai wondered if it was all a dream
when guards came to tell him the good news, then fed and
bathed him, dressing him in the king's robe.

So it happened that the citizens of the royal city saw a
most surprising sight that morning: Haman, the man many
of them feared and hated because of his power and wicked-
ness, leading a beautiful stallion bearing the royal seal. And
on that horse was riding a scribe many of them had seen at
work in front of the palace, who now wore one of the
king's own robes! Mordecai smiled weakly and nodded to
the people as Haman hoarsely shouted, "This is what is
done for the man the king delights to honor!"

News quickly spread through the city, and crowds gathered to watch and discuss among themselves what it all
meant—especially the Jewish community, who had heard of
the terrible edict proclaiming their annihilation on the thirteenth day of Adar. But here was a Jew, their friend Mordecai, whom they had known for years, being honored by
the king—and being escorted by a notorious enemy of the
Jews! It was most amazing and mystifying.

When Haman staggered home that evening, he told his
wife and friends it was the worst day of his life. He
described everything that had happened since his audience

with the king. They were trying to comfort and advise him when the king's guards arrived to escort Haman to the second banquet with the king and queen. He protested that he hadn't yet washed the grime of the city off of him, but they hurried him out the door anyway. "The king and queen must not be kept waiting," they told him.

Esther was putting the finishing touches on the evening's banquet when Jesse rushed in to tell her about the astounding events of the day. They both laughed so exuberantly at the turn of events that they could hardly contain themselves.

"Oh, my precious Papa Mordecai!" exclaimed Esther, wiping her eyes. "I am so glad for him, and this gives me courage to carry through with my plan this very night." Her voice had turned serious, and she looked at Jesse and asked him to be praying for her that evening.

"Oh yes, my little Hadassah," he said, his voice low. "I will be praying, and I will also tell Mordecai about it, and he will pray, too."

CHAPTER SEVENTEEN

SO THE THREE GATHERED AROUND THE TABLE FOR another delightful meal Queen Esther had planned for them, this time held in her own private quarters. A maid played a harp, and lovely breezes caught the edges of the wispy curtains draped on each side of the table.

Esther had made sure the servants were instructed to keep the wine out of Haman's reach and to refill his goblet only at a signal from her.

After the last dish had been served and eaten, the king looked at Esther with an encouraging smile and asked, "Now, my queen, what is it that you are wanting? Whatever it is, you can ask for anything, even half the riches of my kingdom."

Esther was silent for a moment, and then she lifted her head and said, "If I have found favor with you and if it pleases Your Majesty, I beg of you to give me my life."

The king sat up straight, a baffled expression on his face.

Esther continued, her voice quivering, "I and my people have been marked for destruction and slaughter. A man has schemed a monstrous plot against us."

Xerxes leaped up from his lounge. "Where is he? Who is the man who has dared to plan such an evil thing?" he demanded, waving his fists in the air.

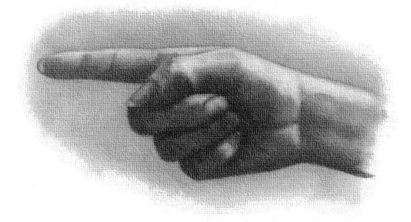

Esther also rose to her feet, and with a dramatic gesture she lifted her hand and pointed to the other side of the table. "The enemy of me and my people is this wicked Haman," she announced. "For I am a Jew!"

The king's face was red with rage, and he whirled around and stomped out into the garden. He needed time to get himself under control, to consider what he would do. His mind whirled as he worked to mentally reconstruct how Haman had tricked him into an evil edict under false pretexts, betraying the power and position he had been given.

Haman was absolutely terrified, and he crept as near to Esther as he could, throwing himself at her feet and begging the queen for his life.

"I . . . I had no idea you were a Jew, Your Highness," he stammered frantically. "There's been a terrible mistake! I did not know." He was now blubbering so hard he could barely talk. "It was just the terrible old Jew that sits at the gate—"

"That 'old Jew' *is my father!*" the queen interrupted Haman's tirade. She turned away from him, and when Haman scrambled after her, he lost his balance and fell upon her just as the king returned from the garden.

"*What?* You will assault my queen in front of my face?" the king shouted. He became even more angry, and he motioned to a nearby guard. The man came over and covered Haman's face with a white cloth, a sure sign that it was all over for Haman.

The guard said to the king, "Haman has built a gallows fifty meters high near his house. The word is that he made it for Mordecai."

The king twisted away from Haman, who was whimpering in anguish on the floor, and ordered, "Take my ring off his finger and hang him on his own gallows!"

That night the evil Haman was hanged on the very gallows which he had built and on which he had thought Mordecai would die.

Now Queen Esther was able to tell her complete story to King Xerxes. She explained to her husband that Mordecai was the one who had been a father to her after her parents had been killed. She brought Mordecai in to introduce him to the king, and he put his signet ring on Mordecai's finger. "You will be my new Master of Audiences," the king told Mordecai. Then he went on to say that he was giving all Haman's wealth to Esther.

Then Esther said to Mordecai, "Would you please manage Haman's estate for me?" At his nod, she couldn't help but put her arms around her father's neck, and they stood there, caught in the swirl of emotions they were feeling—joy at the vindication of their enemy and fear for the future and the edict still facing them.

Then Queen Esther turned from Mordecai and threw herself down before the king, weeping. "Please, my king, my husband, please put an end to the evil plan of Haman!"

The king once more held out his scepter and reached to lift Esther to her feet.

"I beg of you," Esther said as she stood before the king, "to order a new decree overruling the one Haman sent out to all the provinces of the Persian Empire."

"Yes, I will do exactly that," replied the king. He sent for the royal secretaries and instructed Mordecai to tell them just what to write.

Mordecai dictated to the scribes a new decree. On the thirteenth day of Adar, all Jews in Persia would have the right to organize, to fight, and to protect themselves against any group or army that might attack them or their children. Then Mordecai sealed the new decree with the king's own signet ring now on his finger.

The king's stable of fast horses was once again drafted into service, and the royal couriers were soon racing across the surrounding desert to get copies of the new edict to all 127 Persian provinces. The king made it very clear that all the Jews were under the particular protection of the king himself, and any who tried to carry out Haman's wicked decree against the Jews would themselves be killed.

Mordecai promoted Jesse—Hathach—to be his assistant, and as soon as she could, Esther arranged for a joyful family reunion with his grandmother Rachel and his parents.

"Would you come here to the palace and live with me, Mama Rachel?" Esther asked the woman who had been like a mother to her.

Rachel looked around at the elegant surroundings, then smiled and shook her head.

"No, no, I want to stay in my home where I've lived most of my life, Hadassah dear—you may be queen, you know, but you'll always be Hadassah to me," Rachel added with a knowing smile. "But I wouldn't mind visiting you now and then, especially if my Jesse can join us occasionally." Esther was very happy to agree to that with a hug and a smile.

Mordecai rode out into the streets of the royal city, again dressed in royal robes and wearing a beautiful gold crown, and wherever he went, the Jews were celebrating their deliverance. Even people of other nationalities lined up to become Jews so they could get in on the king's special favor!

When the thirteenth day of Adar arrived, the nobles and administrators of the king in each province even helped the Jews defend themselves from the few who were foolish enough to try to attack them.

The day after the thirteenth of Adar was a day to rest, to celebrate, and to give gifts of food to one another and especially to the poor. Queen Esther and Mordecai announced this would be an annual event, the Feast of Purim, when all Jews everywhere would remember their salvation from destruction.

That evening Queen Esther and Mordecai stood on the balcony of the palace, looking out over the royal city. The sun was nearly down below the horizon in the west, and a refreshing breeze cooled the air around them. Neither of them spoke for a while, and then Esther turned to her father.

"Oh, Papa," she said, linking her arm through his as they watched the lingering sun. "I am so thankful to God for all the things you taught me, all the ways you were an example to me of faith and courage."

"Hush, my daughter," Mordecai responded. "I'm afraid the times I failed you—and, yes, failed God—are far more than those when I obeyed God and followed the teachings in the Holy Scriptures."

Esther hurried to answer, "But the times I remember are the ones that have given me hope—hope that God was with me even when I was not aware of it. And that He would use a simple Jewish girl to accomplish what He wanted."

The two turned to go back inside. Mordecai stood in the doorway a moment, then smiled and joked, "If you hadn't been brave enough to approach the king even at the risk of death, I might still be sitting down there at the palace gates with my pen and parchments." Father and daughter both laughed as the door closed behind them.

The truth was that if Queen Esther had not been brave enough to risk approaching the king, all the Jews, including Mordecai and even Esther, would have been destroyed.

Mordecai was second-in-command to the king. He became a person of great influence in the land of Persia, and his fellow Jews held him in high honor because he worked for the good of his people and spoke up in the court for their welfare.

And because he had raised a little orphan girl, Hadassah, to become Esther, Queen of Persia.

THE FEAST OF PURIM

THIS FEAST COMMEMORATES THE TIME WHEN THE
Jewish people living in Persia (today's Iran and Iraq) were
saved from extermination by the faith and bravery of a
beautiful young Jewish girl. The word "purim" refers to
"casting lots" (something like throwing dice) and to the lot-
tery method Haman used to determine the date for the
planned massacre. The thirteenth day of Adar usually
occurs in March, a month before Passover.

A Purim tradition is the eating of a fruit-filled pastry
called "hamantaschen," or Haman's Hat, possibly a refer-
ence to the cloth of death laid over his head when he and
his wicked plan had been exposed by Queen Esther.

Here is a recipe for hamantaschen:

$^2/_3$ cup butter or margarine
$^1/_2$ cup sugar
1 egg
$^1/_4$ cup orange juice (no pulp)
1 cup white flour
1 cup wheat flour
Preserves, fruit butters, or fruit pie fillings

Blend thoroughly after each addition: butter and sugar, egg, orange juice. Blend in both flours, $1/2$ cup at a time. Refrigerate batter overnight or at least several hours. Roll out the batter as thin as possible between two sheets of waxed paper lightly dusted with flour. Cut out 3- or 4-inch circles, top with a tablespoon of filling of your choice, then fold the sides to make a triangle, overlapping the sides so only a little filling is visible. Squeeze the corners firmly together so they remain sealed during baking. Bake at 375° F for 10 to 15 minutes until golden brown. Enjoy—and think about Queen Esther and her bravery in the face of death!